Constable Katya Investigates

Contents

CHAPTER ONE: DEATH BY THE DNEIPER
-A Constable Katya Investigation-

PART I

I'm enjoying kasha and burnt sausage for breakfast, when I catch the first report of Tatty Akkuratney's murder on my kitchen TV. I don't recognize the victim's name, but it turns out she's a moderately well-known YouTube blogger. A frail old babushka discovered the body as she was taking out her tiny sack of trash, and the camera pans to a dumpster and a cracked toilet beneath a leafless tree.

The crime is especially pitiful since the girl's hands were chopped off.

While I'm listening for details, my cat Masha takes advantage and leaps onto the table to snag my sausage. What can I do? She's barely out of kitten-hood and totally amoral. If anyone knows how to train a cat, please write me – Constable Katya Kondrashov, Police Department, Kiev, Ukraine.

Well, that's the end of Tatty Akkuratney, but it turns out it isn't, because when I reach work I'm called into Commander Shulikov's office. The Commander says he's pulling me off patrol and assigning me a desk, and while it's clear I'm being disciplined, it's unclear why.

My infractions are like guppies; it's hard to single one out.

"I'd like you to assist a team of detectives with phone tips and travel arrangements," explains Shulikov. He hands me a departmental credit card. "Exercise your best judgement, Constable."

"Which detectives?" I ask.

"Mister Zubov and Mister Volodney," answers Shulikov.

Everything shifts. I'm thrown into a parallel universe where things actually work out for Katya Kondrashov. Mister Sanya Zubov has amazing grey eyes, and shoulders like a shot-putter, and I have a gigantic crush.

Guess what? They're investigating the murder of videoblogger Tatty Akkuratney. "Thank you for the assignment, sir, I'm pleased to help out," I tell Commander Shulikov as I leave.

The other detective is Misha Volodney, and when I report for duty, Volodney confirms that they've been deluged with phone tips. Then he adds that we're heading out, grab a set of keys from car pool, you're driving.

"I'm baby-sitting the phones," I answer.

Volodney grins. "Keys, Constable." I brighten up. Who am I to argue with a superior officer?

Volodney gives me a location on Klovsky Descent, and while I'm chauffeuring him there, I ask why we're not sifting the crime scene for clues.

"We haven't got a crime scene," replies Volodney. "Not yet."   He explains that although the body was dumped under a tree, the victim was murdered elsewhere. Possibly by Pasha Bulychuk, who was put on trial last year for raping and strangling a tram driver by the name of Natalia Bulgarin, and removing her arms with a hacksaw, not necessarily in that order. Pasha is the son of Deputy Bulychuk, of the Ukrainian parliament, which, we are told, had nothing to do with Pasha's subsequent acquittal.

"Where's Mister Zubov?" is my next question, referring to good-looking Sanya.   "Talking to the girl's family," says Volodney, offering me a cottage cheese donut from a paper bag. I'm guessing Volodney's closing in on forty, and I note with approval that his suit is clean and freshly ironed.

****

I've never visited a Deputy of Parliament's home, but as soon as we're inside I can tell that this Deputy is divorced. It's a single male's playpen, twenty stories up, with a glass-top bar and rows of floor-standing, dancing-bubble fountains. There's gold plated plumbing on the sinks and the fridge holds rows of bottled Perrier, and the freezer is stocked with vodka and cheesecake. Volodney and I are poking around after the concierge lets us in. No sign of the Deputy, nor of Pasha, the acquitted amputation artist.

A knock, I open the door and admit Detective Sanya Zubov.

Let me stipulate that Zubov's dual shades of brown hair, like two quality chocolates –a light Bavarian chocolate, melted and poured over a dark, Russian Babaevsky, and then swirled but not blended - have nothing to do with my feelings toward him. Nor does Sanya's athletic body inside the crisp suit, which I can only imagine.

What attracts me to Detective Zubov is the fact that he's absolutely, at all times, *in charge.*

He ignores me. "What have you turned up?" he asks Volodney.

Volodney tells him that the Deputy has just left a committee hearing and will arrive shortly, and that son Pasha is skiing in the Carpathians, according to the concierge. Furthermore, there's late word that the dead girl Tatty Akkuratney had a boyfriend, also a video blogger, who only hours ago flew to Moscow, Russia, according to his mother.

"By the way, this is Miss Kondrashov, who's been loaned from patrol." Zubov brushes past me, and Volodney and I follow him to a sliding glass door, which Detective Zubov draws back to admit mild March air. We all step onto a balcony and look twenty stories down.

I don't know if Zubov is pondering the case, or admiring the Olympic Stadium, but I anticipate his insight. Down below there's scant snow for the first week in March, and the weather bureau says not much in the Carpathians, either. In fact, the ski resorts have crocuses popping up, so it seems likely that "hacksaw" Pasha hasn't journeyed to the Carpathians to ski, but to find a rock to hide under. It also looks suspicious that Tatty Akkuratney's video blogger boyfriend has chosen today to fly to Moscow, but maybe that's just me.

"Check out the victim's YouTube posts," Zubov tells Volodney. "See if she mentioned anyone suspicious. I've already interviewed her parents; they're in the dark. Tomorrow morning we're flying to Moscow to interview the boyfriend."

"Me too, sir?" I ask. Mister Zubov appears uncertain whether he heard a voice from the TV, or a neighbor behind the wall. He focuses on Volodney. "Take a statement from the Deputy when he arrives," he says.

Then he's gone, past the bubble columns and out the door, and I swoon a little against the balcony railing.

"Careful," says Volodney.

****

I'm packing for Moscow. I rent the second floor of my brother-in-law's house, and I leave the door propped open when I'm out, so my cat Masha will have the company, and hopefully, the caregiving of those on the lower level.

From downstairs I catch the keening of my three-year-old nephew, Klem. Full name Klemente (if you're wondering) and every time he cries I hear profound betrayal. My sister says little boys cry more frequently and with less provocation than little girls, and I wonder what happens to that impulse when they're older -maybe it goes away, maybe it doesn't, but if it doesn't, it explains a lot.

"I *knew* that poor girl!" says my sister minutes later, when I stand beside her at the stove.

"You didn't know her, you watched her on Periscope," I say. I've arrived in time to prevent her eating all the crispy skin from the roast duck, which is everyone's favorite part. Her own children sit at the table just four feet away, impatiently waiting sustenance, unaware of their mother's selfish behavior.

My sister sniffles. "You're callous. Otherwise you wouldn't have chosen a career with the police."

I don't have an answer to that, since it may be partly true.

"I hope you catch him," says Anna. "Not you personally, that would be too dangerous." She lifts a knife and slices the wings off the duck.

PART II

Eight AM, we're boarding for Moscow and I'm with the men, having booked tickets on a department card provided by Commander Shulikov. Six months from now someone will demand to know who authorized business class (me), and while they're fretting over the expense, they may forget to ask who authorized a lowly constable to go at all.

I've never been to Russia, and I plan to promenade across Red Square, for that *I'm-at-the-center-of-the-world* thrill, and hopefully to snap pictures of me and Sanya Zubov linking arms.

I also have a list of gifts for my niece and two nephews compiled by my sister, which I know she expects me to pay for, and they're not all souvenirs. There are certain anomalies. *Something for the winter blues,* Anna has scribbled at the end.

****

"What did you find out?" inquires Sanya Zubov, leaning across the aisle. Volodney shifts in the window seat like a child needing a pee. I remember that Zubov asked him to check out Tatty Akkuratney's videos, and after a pause I violate my cardinal rule, which is to keep my mouth shut.

"Nothing there, sir," I reply on Volodney's behalf. "She liked to stroll through the parks alone, while she filmed herself chattering. Not a risk taker, just oblivious. If anyone was tailing her and brandishing a hacksaw, she overlooked it."

"It was a long shot," says Sanya. "Good work, Mister Volodney," he adds.

"Thank you, sir," says Volodney.

We land in Moscow noonish, Mister Volodney flags a taxi and directs the driver to the Brighton hotel. This is where video blogger Philip Deruga is holed up, according to Russian Immigration, and since most young men without a day job are night owls, we may catch him before he rolls out of bed. The taxi driver asks Sanya Zubov, who occupies the front passenger seat, "That's something, isn't it? About the Akkuratney girl?"

Beside me, Volodney's eyebrows twitch, but I'm not surprised that news of our local murder has reached Moscow. All Ukrainian video bloggers employ the Russian language, and Tatty was no exception. They'd be stupid not too, it's a huge audience.

A news kiosk occupies the sidewalk next to the Brighton, but there's nothing about our victim, it's all Dicaprio, Dicaprio. Russians have a big fat crush on Leonardo DiCaprio, and he's just snagged his first Oscar, so it's a national holiday here. Zubov shows his credentials at the desk, and we go upstairs.

Tatty's boyfriend, Philip Deruga, is known in Ukrainian street slang as an extreme roofer. He scales bridge supports, or hangs off the edges of tall buildings by his fingertips. He also balances on the roof of speeding commuter trains, and strips to his underwear and rides a toilet down the street on a skateboard, and tasers and maces his numb-nuts friends. He films it all with his GoPro, and posts it to YouTube, and he's not just famous in Ukraine, he's a phenomenon in Russia too. Deruga's a big earner, not only from YouTube, but from advertising deals as well.

I hear all this from my sister Anna, who's stuck with three preschoolers all day, and has sacrificed her youth. (You know I'm smiling)

Upstairs, Volodney knocks gently on Philip's hotel door, not wanting to spook him, but in vain. We return to the Brighton lobby without speaking to our person of interest; nor did the desk clerk notice him go out, so we buttonhole the doorman, who says he hailed Deruga a cab and overheard the words Moscow City. Sanya Zubov perks up after hearing this; Moscow City is a modern cluster of skyscrapers, boasting dance clubs, sushi bars, and high-end clothing boutiques, and perhaps Sanya imagines he'll spot a fashion model. On the side walk I say I need the ladies', and everyone looks around for a MacDonald's. We find a Starbucks a block away. I use the toilet, and when I come out the detectives are sipping Kenyan and ready to leave. They haven't ordered me anything, but I tell myself I'm a grownup, so don't sulk.

"If there's a mall in Moscow City, that's where he'll be," says Volodney. This isn't deductive reasoning; he's simply stating the obvious. Nobody loves a shopping mall more than a Ukrainian. He nudges me with an elbow, and passes me a Starbucks bag with a chocolate croissant.

****

The shopping mall in Moscow City is dazzling, we all pause in the atrium, momentarily transfixed by a fountain jetting water five stories high. "He likes to wear a Dynamo football jacket," I tell the others, "it's his trademark." They pretend they already know, so I don't add that Philip Deruga recently dyed his hair blond, and doesn't resemble the photo the two of them are passing back and forth. I know Philip is now blond because my sister Anna, who has a desperate, adolescent crush on Philip Deruga, told me so.

"Food court," says Volodney.

I believe there are richer hunting grounds, but you know me, mouth shut.

The food court's stadium-huge, and we've hit the lunch hour. Soon both men are not really searching at all, unless you count the menu board at the Teremok blini and borsht counter.

I'm getting impatient, so I say, "He's hanging out in the arcade."

No one reacts. "If he's not at the arcade he's in the Converse store, buying the most expensive sneakers they have," I elaborate.

I point to a directory mid-concourse, and after getting our bearings we ride the escalator three floors up.

There's a mechanical bull at the entrance to the arcade, only no one's riding him at the moment, and he's paused with his ass in the air. Beyond the bull there's a maze of gaming consoles, but it's a school day, so not much action.

Philip Deruga is working out his grief over Tatty Akkuratney on a trampoline the size and shape of a tennis court, in his stocking feet, surrounded by ball pits, and watched by an awed group of fans. There's also a separate contingent of *gopniks*, members of a thuggish Russian subculture, the sort of urban trash who love Deruga's lame brain antics. Philip's wearing his blue sports jacket and filming himself with a selfie stick as he hops around on the trampoline with a pair of girl fans, and when Mister

Volodney whistles and waves him over, he retorts with obscenities and then pivots the camera to himself to capture a delighted grin.

Volodney removes his shoes, and Sanya follows suit, and the two men make their way to the head of the floor, part the black netting at the entrance, and somersault onto the trampoline to the jeers of Philip's fans. I step back and wait as the detectives bounce tentatively, and then Sanya executes two forward flips toward the end of the trampoline where Philip and one of his girl fans link hands, still filming, and cavort in a circle.

As Sanya plants his landing, Philip's girl admirer shrieks and kicks ferociously, fails to connect, and bounces into the ball pit and sinks from view. Volodney and Sanya each grab a Deruga appendage and haul him toward the netting at the top.

I see an opportunity to help, but a gopnik thug blocks me and shoves me into the ball pit. I panic because I'm head down in six feet of rubber balls, and I thrash around trying to find daylight. The gopniks converge on Sanya and Volodney, Volodney gets cracked across the face, and Sanya, like me, falls into the rubber balls trying to hold onto Philip, who shrugs out of his shiny blue jersey just in time, switches camera hands as he does so, grabs his shoes, and runs away giggling. And filming.

Sanya pulls himself out of the ball pit, brandishing the jersey like a trophy, and Volodney offers me a hand.

We regroup in the food court and order kvass, blini, and borscht at Teremok. "He didn't commit murder," opines Volodney. "He's enjoying the easy life; he's a punk, not a killer."

Sanya nods in equable agreement.

I seem to be the only one who's bummed. I feel that I should remind them why we're here, that a girl was found dead between a dumpster and a cracked toilet bowl, but after struggling with the sentiment, I say nothing.

"Tomorrow we go skiing," decides Sanya Zubov, brushing beads of red caviar from his lips with a fingertip. I assume he's planning to tackle Pasha Bulychuk, hacksaw boy, who's next on the list of suspects.

"You'll make travel arrangements," he says, making eye contact with me.

Suddenly I'm not bummed anymore; intoxicating chemicals are flooding my brain, and I'm floating.

****

At home, I give the kids the candy I bought at the Moscow airport; it's the same stuff Anna buys them at Cash and Carry, but they're thrilled it's been flown to them all the way from Moscow.

I hand my sister a wrinkled grocery bag.

"What's this?" She wrinkles her nose as if she might find something jokey and dubious, but inside is Philip Deruga's signature Dynamo sports jersey. I spend the next five minutes convincing her it came directly from her idol's skinny torso, and it's loaded with Deruga molecules.

"No way," says Anna. She doesn't ask whether she can keep it. She has a look of naked happiness as she rubs it against her cheek, then she scuttles away in her flip flops. The children's faces swivel toward me as if I've spooked their mother, wanting an answer, chewing gummies. Klem decides he's been slighted, and blubbers angrily.

****

Volodney calls just as my cat Masha and I are getting ready for bed. The detective's having no luck locating Pasha Bulychuk, since ski resort management has a confidentiality policy, and even the promise of a hefty bribe has fallen flat. Deputy Bulychuk is keeping little Pasha under wraps.

"Which hotel is priciest?" I ask, pulling on my bedtime woolen socks.

"Hold on."

While I wait, I google Deputy Bulychuk/divorce, and find out that his ex has remarried and is living in Odessa. Volodney comes back and says, the Hotel Ibex at the Bukovel resort, adjacent to chair-lift number three. They offer a package deal for two, air fare, three days and nights, with complimentary meals, sauna and facials for 20,000 Hryvia.

Volodney's tone is neutral, but 20,000 Hryvia is what I make in a month, so I'm fighting the despair that I feel when I'm reminded what a cozy life other people have. "Give me the phone number," I say.

I call Hotel Ibex and tell them I'm Lydia Gavrilov, Pasha Bulychuk's mother, and be so kind as put me through. I sense hesitation on the other end so I add, "According to my online account, the boy is running up exorbitant charges on my Platinum Visa, and right now my thumb is hovering over the 'don't authorize' option."

"One moment, Mrs. Gavrilov."

Moments later I hear a slurred voice on the other end, "Yeah?"

"Vanushka," I say, "it's Katya. Good news – I'm pregnant!"

On the other end I sense a struggle to process. I believe Pasha thinks it's room service, because he orders sushi and a deluxe pizza.

I hang up and call the front desk back, book two package deals at 20,000 each and charge it to the Kiev Police Department.

****

During the night it snows. In the morning my cat Masha sits wide-eyed at the window, and I'd love to know what she's thinking, but maybe she's just hypnotized. The weather boffins have correctly forecast snow, it's the 'how much' part they've miscalculated. At the airport it's falling heavily, but we lift off on schedule. This time I'm sitting next to Sanya Zubov, who's wearing a pinstripe grey suit, blue tie, black shoes with a high gloss, and my breathing is deep and calm, because I'm concentrating on a solitaire game on my phone.

"We should rent skis," Volodney is saying, "in case there's a downhill pursuit."

"Snowboards have more control," answers Sanya. He leans across me, stretching out a muscular hand to demonstrate edge pressure, and for an instant his face is centimeters from mine. Have I mentioned his eyelashes? At this point I'm going to keep my overheated thoughts to myself until we land.

There's a mini bus waiting as we touch down; four others who've bought the package deal squeeze in behind us, and we're all driven over rutted roads of mud churned with fresh snow, where green and blue houses wait behind tall, occluding fences, and here and there bony dogs watch without hope as we pass.

Soon we're on a better road, the sort paid for by private enterprise and not government, climbing steeply through birch and pine.

The Ibex Hotel in Bukovel is rustic alpine, and by rustic, I mean it was probably built three years ago. There's a main building with service facilities, surrounded by private lodges at discreet distances, ringed by trees. We check in, then are led along a walkway to an A-frame Swiss-type chalet, where we unpack our bags. It's been agreed that we'll need to go native in order to assess the situation.

I spend some time changing into ski slope attire, and when I return to the living area both men are absent, but eventually I encounter Volodney in the main building scrounging leftover breakfast buffet in the dining room.

"Pasha Bulychuk's already on the slopes," he says.

"Where's Mister Zubov?"

On cue Sanya Zubov enters, lugging a snow board from rentals, wearing a white and blue ski jacket with trendy trapezoid patterns, goggles strapped to his helmet.

"Two bodyguards," reports Sanya.

I believe we've assumed Pasha Bulychuk would have security, but it's suddenly clear that sitting Pasha down under a dangling light bulb will entail strategizing.

"We'll get to him when he hits the john," suggests Volodney.

"He'll deny everything and his bodyguards will alibi him," I point out.

"Pasha's not an easy target," Zubov agrees. "We need to question his security people. If one of them has a police record, we can twist his arm."

"We wait until dark and follow them from the dining room," advises Volodney. "We'll separate one from the pack."

Sanya considers. "Not bad, but we can do the same on the slopes."

We encounter all three men in a coffee shop near the chair lifts, where I get a good look at Pasha. You can tell rich men by their teeth, and Pasha has a megawatt smile. He dabbles in the music business with Papa's money, and wanders in and out of the fashion world, and if I've given the impression he's just a youngster, I apologize. He's in his thirties, with small dark eyes, groomed facial stubble, not very tall, but sinewy and athletic. Girls looking for someone to drop a good word with a designer or music producer find him useful, so he's rarely without company. Obviously the ones who read the news are going to steer clear.

Natalia the tram driver was still alive when her arms were sawed off.

Going up on the chair lift is breathtaking, there are mountain ranges to the east and snow-frosted spruce on my right, but I soon realize how close-to-vertical the slopes are. To be truthful, I'm better at cross country than downhill, but it's past time to bring that up.

When we reach the top of the run, Pasha and his security detail are ahead of us, waiting on the sidelines for a turn. Everyone fiddles with goggles, and as soon as they push off, we follow.

I hurdle downward. They say the moon falls endlessly toward earth, and always misses, and I'm hoping for the same luck. Below me I notice Sanya Zubov suddenly drop his stance on the snowboard as he veers left and collides with the trailing bodyguard, and both disappear into a stand of trees. When Volodney and I catch up, Sanya's trying to revive the man, who's spread-eagled, non-responsive, possibly concussed.

Volodney fishes an ID out of the guy's parka, and I check police records on my phone. The bodyguard's ex-army, has traffic tickets, but no real pressure points.

Zubov's not giving up. He rubs snow on the guy's face, brings him around, and he and Volodney soon have him upright, while they pat him on the back and assure him he'll be fine. Does he remember what day it is? Who's the president of Ukraine? What about the night Tatty Akkuratney was murdered?

The guy haltingly repeats what is obviously a prepared story, Pasha was with an aspiring transsexual model named Doronina, all afternoon and evening; she'll be happy to swear to it.

Sanya tries an unexpected tact. "Your fought the Russians, in Donbass. You're an honorable person. Help us out."

Maybe the guy is woozy from concussion, maybe the appeal to honor has an effect, maybe he really did fight the Russians, but eventually he admits that Pasha was alone on the night of the murder. He assumes Pasha was in the bubble-fountain penthouse at the time, but Pasha's given security the slip before, it could have happened that night too.

Volodney and Zubov exchange grim looks. Pasha Bulychuk lacks an alibi.

I phone for a rescue, Volodney waits with the bodyguard until they bring up a sled, while Sanya and I ski down the mountain together, in a manner of speaking. "Skiing down together" is accurate in the most literal sense, and I'm not amending it.

Pasha and his remaining bodyguard are waiting near the chairlift, possible debating whether to return for their missing comrade. Sanya urges them into the coffee shop, assures them their guy is receiving medical attention, and apologizes for the collision. Meanwhile I order myself cocoa and a pumpkin tart.

After dinner Sanya decides to head back to Kiev, so we wait in a frigid train station below the mountain - toilets without doors, no refreshments - until nearly midnight. No one complains, we're cops, it's just another day. When we get back to Kiev dawn is breaking, the snow has stopped, I'm nauseous from coffee, and I've lost money at cards.

PART III

It's up to Commander Shulikov to decide what happens next, but there is no "next", the Tatty Akkuratney murder investigation trails off, interest evaporates because Pasha Bulychuk did it for sure, and he's untouchable. In the weeks that follow I run into Sanya, and then Volodney, and Volodney is pleased to see me, but we quickly run out of conversation. Sanya is polite, but on his way somewhere else, and that's fine because we're essentially of different species. Our children would end up in zoos.

I continue to believe that no girl deserves to be dumped in the trash, so I don't forget Tatty, even when I'm back on patrol, and one day I run into Philip Deruga again.

****

Street Shoes is a hole in the wall selling popular sneaker brands, plus accessories, and it's not cheap. I'm looking for a pair of Nikes for my younger brother Slava, who's twenty-two and dresses like a twelve-year-old. It's not Slava's birthday; but I've been neglecting him, and I'm feeling guilty. Anyway, in comes Philip Deruga.

Deruga helped popularize Street Shoes on his YouTube channel, and he likely gets discounts if he bothers to ask.   The tiny shop is jam-packed after he comes pounding up the stairs with a half dozen friends. Philip struggles to squeeze by me at the Keds rack, but I snag his arm.

"Tell me about Tatty Akkuratney," I say.

"Weren't you in Moscow?"

I'm surprised he noticed, but he probably has me on video.

"Somebody made off with my Dynamo jacket," he complains.

"One of the gopniks," I say.

"You should be looking into that. My jacket."

"That's for the Russian Police," I tell him.   I can't believe that's his concern. "What about Tatty?" I ask.

He blinks. "I didn't touch her," he says. "We broke up weeks before."

"Before…?"

"Yeah, before."

"What else?"

"She showed up at a fan meeting in Independence Square; we talked and she took off with somebody. I don't know who."

One of the girls says, "Alexei Keks." Laughter follows, all the groupies repeat the word "keks", and there's more laughter. It's a popular kids' word that's recently emerged, it sounds funny and cool, and means cupcake. I pay for Slava's Nikes and leave with an altered mindset, no longer worried about placating my brother.

I'm looking for Alex Cupcake.

****

The nuclear plant in Zaporizhia is known for storing radioactive waste in the open air, and for all you connoisseurs of urban charm, there's smokestack industry as well. Frankly I'm not keen to visit, but on the train a retired Zoporizhian gentleman assures me it's a perfectly adequate place to live; he fishes for pike in the Dnieper River on fair-weather mornings, buys flowers and a rye bun for his wife on return, and he admires Putin. At that point I realize he's senile, so without being rude I shift my attention to the window view.

As it turns out, I'm utterly taken by Zoporizhia from the moment I leave the station in a cab; I'm in love, I feel as if I'm returning after a prolonged absence. My fake nostalgia is a combination of the familiar and the strange, it's Kiev only smaller, but best of all, it's full of people who've never pissed me off. I dab at my eyes. (I react the same when I go to Lvov.)

Alex Cupcake is Alex Poporechney, and his last known address is here in Zaporizhia. I've watched several of his YouTube videos; they post every few days, but recently there's been nothing. The blogs didn't stop on the day Tatty Akkuratney died, but a few weeks previous. He's a sweet-faced nineteen-year-old, with medium length, light colored hair which he's constantly running his hand through, and his videos are of two types: meeting friends to chat and drink, or solo in his apartment, where he addresses the camera and updates his subscribers on his personal relationships, and his journey as a videoblogger, and his financial situation, which I gather is dire. (He endured a brief stint at MacDonald's). His following isn't huge. He's determinedly optimistic, but there's an undertone of unease that he may be losing the battle, by which I mean, he may need to abandon his YouTube dream and get a paying job.

The address I have is on Gorky Street just off Lenin Prospect. Lenin is grand and urban, but once on Gorky we're practically in the countryside. I ask the driver to wait while I unlatch a gate and follow a pathway between red and yellow tulips. I knock on the door.

The woman who answers is nicely dressed, soft-voiced and attractive; she's my height but a few kilos heftier. A girl of about three years hangs on her arm.

I ask for Alexei Poporechney, and she tells me she's his mother. I'm genuinely taken aback, she appears barely older than me, so when she asks me my business I abandon the fiction I've prepared and tell her the truth.

"I'm a constable with the Kiev police department and I'd like to ask Alexei about a fan meeting he attended in Independence Square. He may have witnessed something that could aid us in solving a crime."

"What sort of crime?"

"Homicide."

Surprisingly, she relaxes. I'm guessing she was prepared for petty larceny, but it's murder, so it has nothing to do with her Alexei.

"Mrs. Poporechney, do you know why Alex stopped blogging on YouTube?"

"He's busy these days," she says, obviously pleased, but perhaps hesitant to elaborate to a stranger.

"He's working?"

Maternal pride wins out. "He was hired by the company that manages the shipping locks on the river. If he sticks with it, they'll help with engineering school."

I can tell she's been wanting to tell someone, to test this information in the real world, and see if others buy it.

"He's doing well, then. Is he at home?"

"He took a flat with a friend."

"Could I have the address, Mrs. Poporechney?"

As I leave, I glance back, to see if she's gone inside to phone her son. But no, she's stepped out to enjoy the sun, and the daughter is tugging her toward the tulip beds.

****

The cab takes me toward the river; we're not in the countryside anymore, it's urban decay on every side, rubbish swamping the gutters, street walls scarred, shops sealed with plywood. No reflection on Zaporizhia, cities all over Ukraine have problems now. I pay off the cab because my driver has another fare, and then something unexpected happens.

It turns out Mrs. Poporechney lied.

The street door is open but the lift is broken, so I walk up to the fifth, tap on the door of apartment 504, and a Muslim lady answers. She's never heard of Alex. I return to the lobby and find a row of battered mailboxes, but the name Poporechney is not on any of them. I knock on the first floor apartment door which has a view of the street entrance, and intrude on an elderly gentleman's lunchtime. He shakes his head. No Alexei.

I'm baffled. I'm ready to leave when I notice a hallway door, which I assume is a utility closet. I open it, descend a creaking stairway to the basement, arrive at another door. This one doesn't open although it doesn't appear to be locked, so I put my shoulder into it.

"Alexei?"

I reach through the opening I've made, grope for the light switch, pop it up and down.

"It doesn't work," says a low voice.

"Alexei, I'm Katya Kondrashov with the Kiev police."

"Okay."

"Can I come in?"

No answer, so I shove again and wriggle through. Dim light filters through the crud on a sidewalk-level window, but it's murky. A figure curls on the stone floor, wrapped in layers of clothing.

I bump against a stool, and sit down. My eyes adjust. There's no smell other than basement smell; the furnace has been turned off and it'd be quiet if the plumbing weren't rattling. There's an empty water canister standing against a wall but no sign of food.

"What's going on, Alexei?"

No answer. "Alex I'm not here to harm you. I just want to hear your side of the story."

The figure shifts slightly but I can't see a face.

"Alexei, when was the last time you ate?"

A minute passes. Then a whimper.

"Why don't we go out?" I suggest. "It's a beautiful day, we'll get Pepsis and sandwiches, my treat."

More time passes, I'm starting to wonder what my next ploy will be, and then Alex says in a soft voice, like his mother's, "Could you wait outside please? I have to pee."

"Sure. I'll wait upstairs."

The young man who emerges from the basement and climbs the stairway doesn't resemble Alex Cupcake. This is a boy who's wrung every drop of anguish from his guilt, only to learn that guilt replenishes endlessly. The lively energy of the face, so notable in his YouTube videos, is missing, the cheerfulness replaced by gape-mouthed desolation, every physical marker of youth and attractiveness has been ravaged. Alexei Poporechney is a zombie.

He trails after me, we cut across a kids' playground where young men are pelting each other with empty aluminum cans, and a couple of streets further on we arrive at a sandwich shop with a take-out window on the sidewalk. Alexei hangs back with his face tilted to spring sunlight, I order for both of us, and neither of us speaks until I ask if there's a park where we can eat. Then he lopes ahead with frantic purpose, leading me between two monstrously ugly apartment towers, down a metal stairway, through a fringe of young birches, out onto the grassy slopes above the Dneiper.

From these cliffs men are casting fishing lines into the river, and seagulls hover. I don't think it's a park, although perhaps it's city-owned, because the grass has been mowed.

I make myself comfortable, Alex lowers himself to his knees close by, rips open the wrapping on the sandwich I hand him, scarfs it down, then gulps Pepsi before eyeing my sandwich, which I surrender.

I wonder if he intended to starve himself down in the basement, his final, half-baked Cupcake plan, now just one more plan that didn't pan out. In a moment he's going to realize he doesn't have a back-up.

I'm also curious to know if he cut off Tatty's hands to shift suspicion to the infamous hacksaw killer, but Alexei and I have only just met, and it seems oddly impolite. He's in a delicate state. I doubt he functions normally these days, and his next revelation bears me out.

He chews and smiles. "I asked the gods for help," he tells me finally. He nods toward the big island that cleaves the Dneiper. "The wind was bitter cold, and I didn't wait for an answer."

I recall from high school history that Khortytsia island, which we sit facing, is the home of pre-historic sculptures of our ancestors' gods.

"After that, I tried to outrun him," he tells me finally. "I thought if I ran fast enough I'd leave him behind."

I think he was trying to outrun Alex Cupcake, but I don't know for sure, because Alexei Poporechney has run out of things to say. His animation fades, the chewing slows, and bits of food dribble from his sandwich wrap. Finally, the remainder of his meal spills into the grass. The gulls swoop in, shrieking and thrashing, pleased that we haplessly squander what is ours.

I rise, nudge Alexei to his feet; he holds out his hands like a child, and I slip on the cuffs.

****

It's late before I pull on my woolen bedtime socks the following night, and my cat Masha is waiting to see which side of the bed I'm tending toward, so she can claim it first. I take a moment to think about events.

It's all a pity, but I don't know who to feel sorry for, not Alex who's in the hell he deserves, and not Tatty Akkuratney. Tatty's lights went out forever when she died, and all the pity in the world won't help her.

Finally, I rarely feel sorry for myself; it saves a lot of fuss.

From below, Klem howls, brother Vanya joins in, and my hands clench as I wait for my sister to comfort them. I realize I feel sorry for all the blameless children who wail in anguish, because they've been ignored, or scolded, and everything is too difficult.

I want to tell them it'll get better, but I suspect it never does, not for some.

CHAPTER TWO – IVANA IVANOVA
-A Constable Katya Investigation-

PART I

The Penguin Club is composed of hearty members of the Kiev Police Department who take a dip in the Dneiper on New Year's Day. I signed on because my sister Anna, who's a stay-at-home mom and jealous of my independence, told me I'm a taker and not a giver. She means I cruise the city in a patrol car, sipping energy drinks, while she changes diapers, boils dumplings, settles disputes between toddlers, and by extension, molds the future of Ukraine.

She insists the least I can do is take an ice bath to benefit disabled cops.

As a result, I'm begging people to sponsor me, but it's the holiday season and everyone's tight on funds. Today I find myself cajoling an intern who's wandered into headquarters from the medical examiner's office; he's young and not bad looking. I was going to say too young for me, but that would be discriminatory. (By the way, if you'd like to sponsor me next year, send your generous check to Constable Katya Kondrashov, Police Department, Kiev, Ukraine)

Young Ruslan Omelechko, from the medical examiner's, hands over his spare cash, and wonders if he can dive in the river too. He thinks it's a fun event for a good cause. I say sure, the Kiev Police Department is all about inclusion, and he could be an honorary Penguin for a day. I'm being ironic, but Ruslan asks if I'll sponsor him, and I point out I'd be giving his money back, and he blushes, and excuses himself.

Fifteen minutes later I realize he was hitting on me.

****

That night as I'm reading, my cat Masha begins kneading my chest with her paws, and I get up to check the fridge for treats. My phone rings. "Constable?"

"Yes?"

"I may have information."

I'm lost, I haven't the fuzziest, I never give my number to civilians.

"I was hoping to find my bicycle in unclaimed property," the voice continues, "when I clicked on missing persons, and saw a picture of Viktoria, with your contact information."

Something is tickling my memory, so I'm quiet for a second, then I ask, "Are you referring to our City Outreach website?"

"Yes, ma'am."

Two years have passed, but it all comes back with a jarring clunk, like a soda dispensed from a vending machine. A woman froze to death near the Podilsko-Voskresensky bridge, a homeless woman no one claimed. Because I found the body, I posted a gruesome post-mortem photo on the cop website, asking for help. I thought I'd used the hotline number, but feather-brain me, I must have listed my mobile.

"Do you have a last name for Viktoria?" I ask the caller.

"Just Viktoria, and I didn't know her personally, but she was a regular at the Liberty Café where I work."

"We assumed she was homeless."

"No, no. Or at least she wasn't lugging a rucksack. She dropped by at eleven o'clock every morning, and she liked a macchiato with honey cake."

Same time every morning, money to spend. She was on a work break, I think. In my head, things realign. Deaths among the homeless are rarely at the top of a cop's to-do list, despite the politically correct blah-blah. In summer, some fall in the river, or knife each other, or are struck down in traffic. In the winter, there's a larger die-off from the combination of arctic air and alcoholism. Pertinent boxes are checked, and a file joins a digital slush pile, but no one follows up.

Now they'll have to.

I continue to question my caller, Miss Jenya Khrystenko, and learn a few details of "Viktoria's" clothing and appearance, which were modest and unremarkable, suitable for a clerk or cubicle drudge. I take Miss Khrystenko's personal info, and tell her someone will be in contact, which is possible but not likely. My feeling is that the label "Transient" will mar the file irrevocably, like a coffee stain, or the inadvertent drip of cherry jam from a blini, and I wonder briefly what I can do, but I already know the answer, which is zilch.

My cat Masha has given up climbing my leg for her treat, she's behind the window curtain, visibly aggrieved, so I give her the herring I was saving for my breakfast.

****

Next morning, I hand off my Viktoria findings to a detective named Ivan, who barely spares a glance. "Maybe she has loved ones waiting to hear," I say lightly, with a nice smile, not wanting to come off as a sarcastic witch, which has caused problems in the past.

"No-can-do, we just caught a case," says Ivan. "Galina Klepikov."

My jaw drops. I can't even process. Galina Klepikov is a *huge* celebrity in Kiev. Thirty years dispensing sappy advice on TV and radio, and she's been murdered?

"When? How?" I ask Ivan, who's grabbing his hat and heading out.

"Dangling from a gantry crane," says Ivan. "Barely recognizable without the orange wig."

That's a gratuitous dig at a venerable figure, but I'll forgive if I can ride along.

"That's not happening," says Ivan.

I join the traffic stream on Naddnipryans'ke, munching a cottage cheese donut, listening to news. There's nothing about Galina Klepikov but the story's going to break momentarily, and the whole town will be nattering.

My phone rings, my dad invites me to the country this weekend; bushels of root vegetables will perish if they don't find a home. My ears prick up. Have you yearned for that elusive, can't-put-your-finger-on-it taste treat? Try turnips in horseradish sauce, and you'll swoon in gratitude to Katya Kondrashov.

I promise my father I'll visit on Sunday morning, and I hint that's there's no need to mention root vegetables to my sister Anna, who will appropriate the entirety without a qualm.

****

Road cops provide an essential service; we keep the homeless out of the tourist areas, call a tow on cars blocking bus stops, and ticket people who smoke in public places. Normally I find the job rewarding, but today I'm a different Katya. I hit the accelerator and blow past three ladies trading punches at a fender-bender, and end up near the auto-rail bridge where I found Viktoria two years ago. Sometimes fate sucks me into the city's deeper currents of evil, and as I leave the car I sense the tug of that insidious maelstrom.

The Podilsko-Voskresensky bridge is a construction boondoggle, plagued by accidents and soft funding; the project is currently "suspended". An unfinished, elevated auto-rail overpass extends into the area west of the river, and is sealed to prevent it being stripped for scrap, but metal thieves and the homeless have breached the fencing so often that no one bothers to fix it any longer. The first time I came here was in response to a complaint about a bonfire. By the time I arrived the fellows from Podilskyi District Hose and Ladder had kicked apart the timbers of the bonfire, and instead of hosing it, were allowing it to burn out.

Today I follow the line of pier columns, past an abandoned backhoe with windows smashed, a bulldozer tagged with graffiti, a prefab supervisory office that appears perfectly normal from the outside, but which is a gateway to an adjacent universe, although not to one of the nicer ones. Twenty meters further I see the inlet and marina off to my left, and this is where I found the dead woman.

Viktoria lay on her side, in a snowy concavity beneath an abutment; she may have stumbled there drunkenly, and paused to rest, and slept. She sparkled everywhere with frost, her face, bare hands, clothing. I shone my flashlight on her face, and snapped her portrait with my Galaxy.

Days went by, I inquired, no one knew of any developments, and me not being a boat rocker, I mostly let it go. I posted the woman's picture on the cops' Outreach site, and last night it paid off, except it hasn't, nothing's changed.

I don't even know if she was examined at the morgue.

I look up between rusting girders, wondering what led her here.

"Good morning!"

I startle. A man with a dog passes; he checks out my uniform, and gives a friendly, complicit wave. He's a trespasser, and so is his dog, and on another day I'd write them both tickets.

PART II

I need a bathing suit in December.

I explain the Penguin Club situation to a harried clerk at Bershka, and after some prodding she searches her stockroom for a half hour, and returns with last summer's rejects. I leave without buying, and with a familiar road cop feeling, that I've added to the frustration of someone else's day, and that the world is an angrier place because of me.

I eat a lunch salad in the Gulliver Mall food court, and check out the dazzling holiday tree, swathed in strands of teensy blue lights, and for five minutes I reconnect with my wide-eyed inner kid. Then I call the medical examiner's office and ask for young- but not too young- Ruslan Omelechko.

He sounds pleased I've called, even after it's clear I'm only begging a favor. I give him a calendar date, he looks it up; it turns out "Ivana Ivanova," -my Viktoria- was shipped to a medical school after ninety days. Yes, there was an examination of the body before it was shipped out, but no autopsy.

Head trauma, fractured pelvis, not inconsistent with a fall.

I'm not grasping this at all. "She didn't fall," I say.

"Body discovered beneath a thirty-meter-high superstructure."

"Discovered by me. She didn't fall," I repeat sharply. "Or jump." At this point I feel indignant on Viktoria's behalf, and I suppose it's in my voice. "The access stairway had been torn down expressly to prevent trespassers climbing up," I tell him, as if he's personally responsible for the report.

There's silence on the other end. If Ruslan Omelechko planned to invite me for beer and a cabbage roll, he's changed his mind.

****

I don't have a private entrance at my brother-in-law's, where I rent the second floor, so I'm exposed to my sister's sticky domestic situation each time I enter or leave. "Here she is!" cries a frantic Anna, towing me into the kitchen. "Tell me everything!"

This is weird, but I'm soon enlightened. "Galina Klepikov!" My sister is horrified, and genuinely grieving, because the stars of Ukrainian TV and YouTube are her second family. I check that my niece and nephews are out of earshot. Vanya is towing a cardboard box with my cat Masha inside, and Nadia is pushing. Masha's eyes glow, she didn't know such fun existed.

"You've already heard everything from TV." I offer Anna the few details I've gleaned, and my sister is soon weeping unashamedly. Her children take note, and their stricken faces swivel in my direction.

I collect my cat, head upstairs, feed her dried food from a bag, which she adores. The day has gone badly, and I'm inordinately grateful when Masha comes to curl up.

****

The old Russian Volga wakens on a sub-zero morning without complaint, it's spent decades in the fastidious care of my father, and he only sold it to me after the illegal annexation of Crimea, when my mother refused to ride in it anymore. I pull onto the quiet street of still sleeping residents. A radio announcer informs me that the owner of Trans-Ukraine, where Galina Klepikov's body was discovered hanging from a gantry crane, has been taken into custody by Kiev police. The reporter plays a snippet from Galina's radio show, in which a trucker calls in to complain he hasn't received wages in three months, and he's thinking of striking. Galina must have been drinking decaf, and still brushing away the morning cobwebs, because she encourages him. I'm not buying it as a motive, but killing trouble-makers is not unheard of.

I think, poor old Galina, the queen of blandishments, strung up as an agitator.

In light snow, I drive east toward Boryspil, my birthplace. My father labored in Boryspil Public

Works until he retired, and my mother still teaches graphic arts at the branch of Kiev University there. A few years back, my parents purchased a house in the countryside, where my father took up gardening, and interfering with neighbors.

As soon as I arrive I see that his pick-up truck has been mounted with a new yellow snowplow, which my father didn't mention on the phone. He wants to surprise me. When my father comes outside I assure him it's amazing, while he demonstrates the plow's hydraulics.

That, my friends, is the likely reason my father asked me to visit. I'm not saying there aren't root vegetables too, but showing off his new snowplow is the main event.

Inside, my mother's grating hardboiled eggs, and the first thing she asks is if Anna is bringing the children for New Year's. She steers me into the TV room to show me an extravagantly decorated tree, which I've already seen, because my mother's texted numerous pics to Anna. The grandkids, and where they spend the New Year, have become a tug of war between the in-laws, and I wisely stay out of it. I ask what's new in Boryspil, and while my father's outside inspecting the engine of the old Volga he sold me, she tells me the following story.

Two months ago the neighbor on the other side of Dad's apple orchard erected a bathhouse, a two story, large scale affair. The noise was disruptive, the size of the project was suspicious, and my father soon discovered that the neighbor intended to rent the premises for special occasions, which would include food and beverages.

In other words, a party venue.

My father filed a complaint, which was dismissed; the man had been granted a variance. There was nothing further to be done, and what remained of the field behind the orchard, which in summer was a fragrant alfalfa meadow, was now to be paved and landscaped.

"It's almost there." My mother raps a wooden spoon on the rim of a pot, offers me a taste without telling me what's in it. It's a savory lamb stew, and I don't need to say a word because I'm in heaven which she can plainly see.

My mother continues. She and my dad, who always crack a window for fresh air, recently awakened to fumes in the bedroom, accompanied by the jarring bass notes of rock music, only to discover that the neighbor was test driving his new bathhouse, and the smoke which came from its four stoves and the cacophony from its sound system would now be the norm. My father, whose anger had been mounting steadily for weeks, jetted steam from both ears, like a cartoon character.

The following afternoon the bathhouse burned to the ground.

Two days later the police came, and both my parents were interviewed. My mother had been at work at the time, my father was plowing snow from neighborhood driveways. The police searched the property, no evidence of incendiary materials was found, and they went away.

In the meantime, there is tension between my parents, because my mother suspects my dad committed arson.

My father comes in from out of doors, and tells me I need to change the oil on the Volga. I was prepared for a lecture on lax maintenance, so I've gotten off lightly.

Lunch is truly delicious, there's kvass with the stew, and pear tart with cream. I repeat what I know about the murder of Galina Klepikov, which isn't much. My mother thinks Galina's set back women's progress by a century, advising them to placate, flatter, settle for less and take a back seat.

On another topic, after being prodded about my social life, I offer up the encounter with the intern from the medical examiner's, Ruslan Omelechko, and I make it sound promising, which it may have been before I derailed it.

Lunch ends, my father pulls his boots back on. "Time to load the harvest," he says. "Come lend a hand."

There's twenty centimeters of fresh snow, and it's still busy falling, enough to draw an intermittent veil behind the orchard trees, so briefly we seem to be at the edge of a forest, although I soon glimpse the ruined framing of the neighbor's bathhouse.

"Is that your handiwork?" I ask, pointing toward the destruction. *If we don't do anything, we can't change anything*, my dad often repeated to Anna and Slava and me, and it's the memory of this warning that prompts my question.

His lips purse, he unlocks the shed door. Blue plastic shelving along the walls supports cardboard boxes, and he opens the first with a yank, so that sawdust spills.

"Mom thinks you should confess, and pay damages."

"She thinks violence doesn't solve anything," my father says dismissively, as if my mother believed in levitation, too. "We all know decisive action can be an efficient solution." He nods toward an impacted stack of bushel baskets, and he holds one end immobile while I wrench the top basket loose. We pack two bushels with a colorful variety of roots and tubers.

"I have an idea why Galina Klepikov was killed," says my father on one of our trips to the Volga.

He's caught me by surprise. "Do tell."

"It's only a theory, but I think people are fundamentally averse to receiving advice," he offers. "It puts them in the position of supplicant, and they resent it."

I've started to worry about my father's mental state, because I'm uncertain if he's talking about Galina Klepikov. "Enough to kill?"

"Things build up," says my father cryptically.

I arrive home late with two bushels of assorted vegetables, a box of my mother's oatmeal cookies, plus four liters of hard cider and two liters of kvass. I enlist my brother-in-law Ilya to ferry it inside, and by the time I remove my boots, my sister Anna is already stowing everything in her larder. "A portion of that was intended for me," I say in a reasonable tone. "I'm the one who drove to Boryspil and back."

Anna shakes her head slowly. "Be serious, Katya," she says.

****

On Monday I'm ticketing cars parked on sidewalks, and I soon have my quota. I call it a morning, circle to the top of a parking garage with a view of the river ferries, and pull out my thermos of soup, along with a tasty piece of raisin babka.

After lunch I begin phoning businesses and organizations near the Liberty Café, where my tipster Jenya works, and within twenty minutes I get a hit on Viktoria. A priest at St Basil's Renaissance Rehabilitation recalls that one of his volunteers left suddenly two years ago; I text him the post-mortem photo of Viktoria; he calls back and says with sadness that Viktoria Andreyevna is nearly unrecognizable without her generous, luminous spirit. He's Reverend Mefody Tuchina, and I can drop in between seven am and four pm. I fire up the engine.

A sign outside St. Basil's soup kitchen says it's open Tuesday's and Friday's, and the counseling and social activity center is active five days a week. The only thing not active is the heating system, and Rev. Mefody wears a parka over a sweater over vestments.

He tells me there's a space heater in his office, and leads the way. We pass a dining room that's empty, then a closed door from behind which resound the unmistakable serve and counter-serve of a ping pong match.

Reverend Mefody's shocked to hear that Viktoria's passed, she was gentle and well liked. And no, he didn't think it odd when she stopped coming, those who volunteer at the Center lead busy lives which often take precedent, he informs me. Her full name was Viktoria Andreyevna Gubenko.

"Did she get along with everyone? Any threats?"

"Nothing of the sort. An angel," responds Reverend Mefody. I find myself staring at his voluminous beard, wondering how he keeps the bread crumbs out, and thinking he could never sneak a cookie without everyone knowing immediately.

Next I ask if Viktoria might have confided in someone at the center.

A silence ensues while Rev. Mefody appears to be choosing his words. "We discourage getting too close to the clients, but Viktoria Andreyevna... had no other way of being. If something happened to someone else, it happened to her, too. Her involvement, however, was limited to teaching chess classes, Monday and Thursday evenings."

This schedule doesn't dovetail with what Jenya Khrystenko told me about a morning routine at Liberty Cafe, and I ask if Rev. Mefody if Viktoria had a day job.

"She was a teller at Credit Agricol Bank," says he.

Now I'm dumbfounded. Far from being a homeless nobody, she had standing in the community. Why wasn't her disappearance duly reported?

I thank the Rev. and I'm on my way out, when I think to ask if I might interview the chess club. He's not keen on the idea. Folks in drug rehab are wary of cops, but I promise to tiptoe and whisper, and while he doesn't give assent, he doesn't say no, either.

The nearest branch of Credit Agricol is on Andrew's Descent, where I learn of a sad little mystery. Viktoria had been hired as a teller, but was let go within three months. She would go missing from her window, and turn up crying in the bathroom. The bank manager is a woman in her sixties, initially defensive, and it's possible she thinks I blame her in some part for Viktoria's death. She takes the time to retrieve an address from personnel, and I'm soon on my way to Volodyrmyrska Street, a few blocks away. I leave my patrol car parked on the sidewalk and hoof it.

Along Andrew's Descent I check out antique shop windows. I'm one of those inexplicable people fascinated by useless old junk, especially if it's cheap. There's a brisk wind blowing, and Volodyrmyrska Street is virtually deserted. In summer these blocks are crammed with art venders, and everyone who's ever set up an easel overlooking the Dneiper makes a killing with the tourists.

The concierge's at Viktoria's apartment building takes note of my uniform, stubs out her cigarette, shows me a suitcase and a cardboard box in a cupboard behind her office. There are no personal effects, not even a passport ID. The concierge asks if she can dispose of the clothing, and I say I'm trying to locate her family, I'll let her know.

"Do you remember any visitors?"

"Her son."

"Can you describe him?"

"Reddish beard. And he was bulgy."

"How's that?"

She lights a fresh cigarette and blows smoke at the ceiling. Then she models a bodybuilder's pose, and taps her arm where a pectoral muscle would be if she had pecs. "Like that," she says.

I'm back in the street when Detective Ivan calls. "Miss Kondrashov, I understand you speak Spanish."

"Un poco. Porqué?"

"No reason." He rings off.

I speak Spanish in a pinch, and I'm wondering what's up, but mostly I'm wondering what's up with Viktoria, so I look up Viktoria Andreyevna Gubenko online, and learn from the Kiev Times that her husband and only son died in a boating accident in Eastern Ukraine. This raises the question of the bulgy muscleman who was visiting her on Volodyrmyrska St, who despite the concierge's assertion, couldn't have been her son. I'm also mulling the image of a vulnerable, emotionally unbalanced woman who came to Kiev after a personal tragedy, and tried to start a new life, and floundered, and no one helped.

After work, I slip on a floral blouse that I wore in high school, plus jeans, parka and knit cap. I take my cat downstairs to play with Anna's kids, then I fire up the Volga and shoot over to Rev. Mefody's.

The chess club at Renaissance Rehab will have a different membership than it did two years ago, and I need to know if there's anyone left over from the old days. I tap on Reverend Mefody's office door but receive no response; I backtrack to the ping pong room where earnest voices are united in prayer, and I poke my head in. Quite by coincidence the prayers come to an end, but I wince at the notion that I've interrupted religious communion; my pagan spirit is already on thin ice. A young priest begins shepherding his charges through a side door into the soup kitchen dining area, where the scraggy poinsettias of past holidays crowd a window shelf, and chess boards await.

The priest looks up with an amiable smile. "New volunteer?"
I evade, rather than lie. "I was hoping to find Reverend Mefody."

"He left for St. Basil's after dinner. Perhaps I can assist you, I'm Pavel Memetov. Everyone calls me Pasha."

"You're a priest?"

"The chess instructor. Did you want to join us?"

There's a reason I mistook him for a priest, and that's because Pavel has an orthodox priest's full beard. He's also endowed with flared leg muscles and swelling chest muscles and corded neck muscles. He's *bulgy.* I remember the concierge at Viktoria Gubenko's old apartment house, tapping her invisible pec.

The others are seated and have begun a match, and I say sure, I'd like to sit in for the evening. Pavel warns that no one "sits in" and he goes off for another chess set and board, and when he returns he introduces me to the group as a new volunteer at the Rehab center, and then rotates to me, and I say, "Hi, I'm Katya."

I don't play chess, but I know how the little guys move on the board, and I can fake it.

Pavel is ruddy cheeked, glowingly exuberant; he oozes young-man hormones from every pore and he's not the reticent type. I don't think it's inflated self-esteem, he seems buoyed by life's gifts, and wants to spread the joy. I ask about the beard and he explains he's been growing it out of admiration for Reverend Mefody.

We open with pawns. He tells me he's a recovering opioid addict, and credits Renaissance Rehab with giving him a second chance, and enthuses over plans to start a goat farm come summer. He's annoying me because his voice booms to include everyone in the room, and I wonder if I can deflate him a bit. I move my bishop, and ask how long he'd been sleeping with Viktoria Gubenko before she went missing.

His fingers tap his queen, and then retreat. He clears his throat a number of times, his face struggles to duplicate the hue of the poinsettia blooms, and his voice drops to a gravelly sotto voce.

"She showed a lot of interest," he says. He assumed it was sexual, he tells me, he made an advance but was rebuffed.

I remember that her son was nineteen, and I can guess why she was drawn to young Pavel, but the reasons have nothing to do with sex.

When she turned him down, she injured his feelings. He cut her off, stopped speaking to her altogether, and soon she relented and submitted. "She was a good looking woman, for her age," he confides without meeting my eye.

I really feel my heart sinking at this point. This dolt took advantage of a woman whose defenses were destroyed when her family died, a person so fragile she frequently fled her teller's window at the bank to cry in a bathroom. My repulsion toward Pavel couldn't be more intense, but at the same time I want to know about Viktoria's final days.

"Did you quarrel?"

"Never. We understood each other perfectly. We often dispensed with conversation altogether, and simply... made love." His confession falters, he realizes Viktoria has turned up again, and not in a pleasant way, but I can't move him off this point, that he and Viktoria didn't fight, and eventually I ask if she was friendly with anyone else at the rehab center. Pavel seizes on the change of topic.

"There was an old fart, a Russian, slippery as a snake, didn't socialize with anyone. He couldn't resist a chess game, though. Viktoria would buttonhole him after class, and the exchanges would become intense."

"Did she explain what they discussed?"

"Primarily the situation on the eastern border. She said his name was Rostik, and he hailed from her birth city of Luhansk. A few weeks after he joined the group, he left and didn't return. He stopped showing up at the shelter at night as well. Someone said he preferred to sleep rough, far from people and buildings."

"Description?"

A shrug. "Trouble with his left hand, it didn't open properly."

"Other than that?"

"Early fifties. Tall. Long hair." His rook takes my bishop. "So she's dead, is that it?"

"Yes, two years ago," I tell him. After that I think he's studying the chess board but then I realize he's praying. I get up to leave, and Pavel jumps up and pursues me into the ping pong room. "I loved her, I would have crawled over broken glass."

I believe him, and that's the moment I start thinking Viktoria didn't lie down drunkenly and freeze to death, but was murdered.

****

My next move is to make inquiries about Pasha's Russian, the reclusive Rostik.

I visit a hippy cafeteria that gives out free food; also a homeless encampment where everyone craps in an open ditch, as well as a shelter run by St. Vladimir Cathedral. Nobody knows Rostik. Eventually I get a call back from the hippy cafeteria suggesting I see a woman who collects and gives out clothing from the basement of their building.

I go twice and find it closed, I finally get the lady's number and ring her. This woman confirms that an older Russian named Rostik has stopped in. His full name is Rostik Zemskova, and the gentleman needs boots, size 45, which she's promised to locate. She's to leave a message with Rev. Vetchislav at St Anthony's when she succeeds.

"I'll purchase the boots, advise him to come at seven this evening, or you'll donate them to someone else."

I check for Zemskova on our police site, but come up empty. I need a line to the Russians, but first I'll need to prove I'm not wasting their time. I head over to Earth Shoes, which I mistake for a discount outlet, and end up paying two thousand Hryvnia for a pair of black winter boots.

Rostik Zemskova shows up early, wearing sneakers on a snowy night. He's sallow in a way that even the winter wind hasn't reddened, and he realizes at once he's been lured into a trap. I assure him I only want information.

"I'd like to find her family; they need to hear" I plead. "If you know anything, please help."

"She didn't have family." He's eyeing the boots, which I'm holding hostage.

"There'll be relatives somewhere. The two of you talked, you must have picked up something."

"She thought she knew me from Luhansk." It's costing him an effort to speak, his jaws clench, he searches for words, and I don't think it's disuse, it's distaste for the act of communicating. "She was mistaken."

I change the subject, and point to his crumpled hand. "Did you slam that in a car door?"

"Combat in Chechnya, years ago."

"You're Chechen."

He bristles. "No, miss, I'm Russian, raised on Russian soil."

This is going nowhere, so I revert to cop mode, and ask for his papers. He's speech may be labored, but his brain is agile, and he's not about to be bulldozed by a woman.

"I don't show papers, not without cause."

"Any reason you chose Kiev to visit?" I ask in a final attempt.

"I'm a tourist. May I have the boots?"

I think the Russians will want him for something or other, but I need a date and place of birth, as well as a patronymic. I ask to see his passport again, but he turns to leave, so I pass him the boots.

He strides out into the snow without trying them on.

PART III

Commander Shulikov calls me into his office. "I notice you're on the Penguin roster this year, Miss Kondrashov. Very, very pleased. Is it true you speak Spanish?"

The commander explains that the housekeeper and grounds keeper at Galina Klepikov's country place are a married couple from Pamplona. Their Russian is rudimentary, their Ukrainian non-existent, and the detectives need fluent and detailed answers. "Report to Mr. Ivan Rudskoy this morning, Constable."

Ivan tells me the trip to Galina's takes place tomorrow, this afternoon he's interviewing personnel at TRU-Vision, where Klepikov worked. I beg cravenly to ride along, and he doesn't say no.

I get an update on the way over. Galina left behind a brother named Vitaly, who lives at her weekend house; he has severe emphysema, can scarcely get out of bed. Contacted by phone, Vitaly claims his sister left Sunday night at the usual time in good spirits.

After her death Galina's car was found parked at her apartment block in Kiev; too bad the door cam in the building entrance doesn't record. I ask about the autopsy. Some bruising over the chest area, cause of death was heart failure, Ivan says, and he adds that she had scratches on her hands, probably a struggle with the assailant.

Ivan's partner interviews the station manager while Ivan and I wait for Alina de la Forêt to finish taping her holiday cooking show.

Alina de la Forêt, also known as Baba Ala, is an iconic Ukrainian. Everyone agrees she's the gold standard for babushkas everywhere, and the likely inventor of semolina pudding with apricot sauce. After the show Ivan and I wait while Alina circulates through the studio audience, after which we get our turn. Her hair is a sleek auburn bob, and she's wearing a white chef's coat pinned with holly leaves, which in spite of forty minutes of on-camera toil, is spotless. Detective Ivan tells her he's a huge fan, he's practically stuttering, but Alina takes it in stride.

Ivan asks if Galina Klepikov had enemies at the TV station.

"Of course not, everyone is heartbroken."

"Did she mention any recent incidents?"

"She quarreled frequently with her neighbors in the country," Alina tells us. I think of my father and his run-ins with his neighbors. "Some nonsense about deer."

I don't feel that Alina de la Forêt is overly grieved by Galina's passing, but it's hard to tell because I'm too star-struck to be objective. As we're leaving an assistant offers us containers of cheese crepes with butter and dill.

When I get home my sister Anna can't believe my good fortune. "Alina de la Forêt! I'd fall on my knees! And you don't even cook!"

"Of course I cook," I retort automatically, although nothing specific comes to mind. I'm afraid to tell her I was given four cheese crepes prepared by Alina de la Forêt's very own hands, and that I ate every one.

***

Mid-morning the next day, we're on our way to Vovk Pagorb, in detective Bumchik's car. Detective Ivan passes back pictures of his wife and kids, all of them radiating familial bliss, and I fall in love with the concept of married life for a few seconds. "You're a lucky fellow," I tell Ivan.

Next he passes back an autopsy photo. "What do you think?"

The picture has been taken before the chest was opened, and Galina's breasts are on display. There's only one conclusion to draw. "Implants," I blurt.

"No kidding," Ivan agrees impatiently, "but what about the bruise?"

Over the sternum I make out the imprint of a cat's paw, or some type of flower, in varying hues of lilac, and there's a particular spot in the center where the skin is broken. "A fist with a ring on one finger," I say.

"Jackpot," says Ivan. "She received a brutal blow to the chest, followed by heart failure."

"All finished with holiday shopping?" asks Detective Bumchik conversationally, glancing into the rearview.

"I'm the last minute type", I say, suddenly thrown into a panic. I've repressed that I need to purchase twenty-five gifts by New Year's, plus a bathing suit.

Galina Klepikov has apparently raked in serious Hryvnia over the decades, and it's on display at her country house. Constructed among wild chestnuts, the wing-like expanses of glass and stone resemble an exotic fledgling preparing for flight, and the windows reflect both river and sky. In the foyer, golden Buddhas and comatose Koi cohabitate beneath elephant ear plants. Beyond lie creamy-beige rooms, with sprawling abstract landscapes in silver frames, and blond hardwood flooring, and configurations of chrome and leather that resemble furniture.

La Señora Saenz is not who I picture when I imagine a housemaid. She's of regal height, cautious in speech, and my impression is that she's no pushover. The husband wears a plain black suit, has beautifully groomed white hair and lacquered fingernails. My modest Spanish turns out to be perfectly adequate.

Galina's brother Vitaly has gone into the hospital overnight for breathing difficulties, but returned this morning by ambulance. He's resting, but able to answer questions, and Detective Ivan heads upstairs, guided by Señor Saenz.

Detective Bumchik and I are ushered into what Señora calls the morning room, which has a breakfast table in a cozy bay overlooking the river, and I can make out a larger dining room through French doors.

We run through a timeline; Galina arrived on Sunday morning, had lunch with her brother, went for a walk, worked on her laptop, used the treadmill, watched TV. She left about nine in the evening.

Next I'm directed by Mister Bumchik to ask Señora Saenz about the marks found on Galina's body. La Señora Saenz shrugs at the mention of bruising, but she has a possible explanation for the scratched hands. During the afternoon on Sunday, Mrs. Klepikov had gone into the woods to feed the *ciervos*, says Señora Saenz. "Ciervos?" I ask. Then I remember Alina de Forêt's statement about deer, and I place my splayed fingers against my forehead, and la Señora nods affirmatively. She thinks Galina encountered a few brambles on the way to look for deer.

Or maybe Galina struggled with whoever punched her in the chest, I think.

Further questioning reveals that Galina, an animal rights activist, frequently squabbled with her neighbor. Galina had directed Señor Saenz to feed the deer in winter months, but this year her neighbor has been shooting them as they pass through his woodlot, and Galina felt she was being made complicit in deer murder. On Sunday Galina had a heated argument with the neighbor, and when she left for Kiev in the evening she was still fuming. This is at odds with the brother's account, who told Ivan in a phone interview that Galina was in good spirits when she left.

Next I ask about Galina's relationship with her brother Vitaly, causing Señora Saenz to arch thick black brows, it's not her place, but when I press, she says they bickered frequently but without rancor, as siblings do.

Any specific bone of contention? Bumchik wants to know.

Señora is growing impatient with our obtuseness. "You must look at the trucking company. They tried to frighten her!" She tells me Galina received death threats from an anonymous caller over advise she gave to a worker threatening to go on strike.

We finish, Detective Bumchik says let's join Ivan, but I say I need to step outside for air, and I'll be along in a sec. As soon as he leaves I ask Señora for directions to the deer-assassin neighbor, and I'm soon following a snowy path along the bluff southward.

****

The neighbor's house is a yellow wedding cake, with white frosting piped up the corners and around the windows. I chat briefly with the lady of the house, who goes inside to fetch her husband.

While I'm waiting outside, I hear a throaty "Hey! Hey!"

I recognize this guy immediately, it's Vova Kovacks from high school, who taught me to identify wild mushrooms in the field.

"I heard you were a traffic cop. What's up, Katya?"

"I'm here about Galina Klepikov. What's your excuse?"

"Hunting and fishing guide to the rich and famous." He grins and puffs out his chest, then nods toward the house. "This one's a client."

"You're looking good, Vova. Any little Vovas yet?"

"Not yet, thank god."

I get serious. "Someone mentioned Galina Klepikov got stuck in a bramble bush over this way."

Vova spreads his hands in a who-knows gesture. "Over the weekend the owner shot two yearling bucks, and Mrs. Klepikov got wind of it. She came charging over to voice outrage."

"Anyone injured?" I ask facetiously.

"Sorry to say, I wasn't present, but I hear the fur flew."

The door opens, we both turn. The owner is a man in his sixties who's had many extra helpings of dumplings over the years, and maybe a glass of vodka this morning. He's in a belligerent mood, and a patrol cop from Kiev isn't worthy of his time.

"What's your authority here?"

"None, sir. I'm assisting in an investigation. I apologize for the intrusion."

"If it's about the stupid Klepikov woman, you can put me at the top of your suspect list."

"If you could tell me what happened Sunday."

"There was nothing to it. The usual accusations of barbarianism, and she spit on me."

There's indignation in his eyes. Even though Galina's dead, he's not letting go.

"She couldn't get it through her head that feeding the deer corn mash inflates the herd, and there's even less natural forage to go around the following year. She wasn't doing a kindness; she was causing more of them to starve."

He's trembling with fury now. "Idiot do-gooders."

My eyes go automatically to his hands, and yes, he's wearing a ring, with a stone. I wonder if it matches the autopsy photo, but I suppose it wouldn't. Whatever happened to Galina, happened in Kiev.

"Thank you for your time sir, you've been helpful." The neighbor waddles back inside and slams his door.

Vova gives me his number. "We'll go mushroom hunting."

"I vividly remember what happened last time."

"All the more reason," he laughs.

"Watch your speed if you come up to Kiev," I say. "Especially if your tail light's busted."

"Hey! Hey!" he replies.

****

I tell the detectives about the neighbor's ring, and the possibility that Galina Klepikov was killed over a dispute about feeding deer.

"For now we're operating on the assumption that she left here under her own power," Ivan responds dismissively. He and Bumchik discuss the brother's interview, most notably anonymous threats against Galina for encouraging strikers at Trans-Ukraine.

"I thought you'd discounted that. They wouldn't hang her on a gantry in their own front yard," I protest.

"The owner's from Kharkov," Bumchik interjects darkly, as if that explained it.

Ivan sighs in agreement. "We need to give the trucking company a second look."

PART IV

We're four days from New Year's and I've purchased only one gift, a dinosaur with remote controls for my nephew Klem, a bit above his abilities as a three-year-old, but not beyond the childish mindset of an adult male, so I figure I've got Klem and his dad Ilya both covered.

I ordered a bathing suit online, and paid for next day delivery, and that was three days ago.

Ivan and his partner have rearrested the owner of Trans Ukraine after a striking employee came forward. He heard the boss say he'd like to throttle the old hen's neck, and he believes the hen in question was Galina Klepikov. The owner hasn't confessed, but Ukrainians never confess to anything.

My nephew Klem draws my portrait one afternoon, my hair is a cross-hatching of several colored pencils, and beneath this beguiling coif I have dots for eyes, and my mouth resembles a pair of wings.

I ask if I can keep it, and Klem coyly consents. I would have asked to keep it anyway, that's protocol with a kid's artwork, but in fact it's reminded me of something which I can't pinpoint at the moment.

****

I'm wondering how to pursue the Viktoria case, and my best bet is lover boy Pavel, who dreams about having a goat farm, and who admires Reverend Mefody to the extent that he's opted for the full blown facial growth. My point is, maybe the best person to talk to Pavel is the Reverend, and I'm mulling this over on a night shift when I get a call. There's a bonfire at the unfinished auto-rail bridge.

It was an earlier bonfire that took me to the bridge the first time.

Again the Podilskyi Hose and Ladder boys have beat me to it, the bonfire embers smolder harmlessly, and the crew is already leaving. I say hi, did you happen to see anyone lurking about when you got here? No one did. I'll just look around then, I say. A couple of them offer to accompany me, but I assure them I'm a big girl.

I look over toward the apartment high rise to the west, thinking someone on a balcony called in the fire, but I can't make anyone out. I have better luck out by the marina, which is where I find Rostik

Zemskova. He's hunkered down among the rocks that line the marina, but my flashlight picks him out, and I say come on up, it's alright, I'm not going to arrest you.

"Want your boots back?" he asks.

"I want to know about Viktoria."

He's shifted toward me on his rock ledge roost, and it's possible he's armed, so I don't repeat my invitation to climb up.

"A woman who'd lost her family was trying to reclaim her life. In spite of everything she was trying to live again, but someone took that away from her."

"You're making me weep."

"I won't arrest you. I've got nothing. You may as well tell me why she took an interest in you."

Now he uncoils and climbs upward over snowy rocks, limber and long-limbed. He's wearing a flat little cap that he removes in an odd display of courtesy when he's standing before me. I'm acutely aware of the darkness and isolation; down in the marina rows of low voltage lamps illuminate a walkway, but the only other light is my flashlight, and a hazy glow from the apartment tower. I tell myself to back away but my feet don't cooperate.

"She told someone you were from her town."

"I'm not. She was delusional."

"She must have given you a reason."

"Like I said, she was crazy. She found out I was Russian, and a ball of yarn began unraveling in her head."

"There are lots of Russians. Too many. Why pick on you?"

"Russian special forces killed her husband and her boy, while they were boating on the river. Shot them down. She thinks they were chasing a Ukrainian recon unit and mistook them."

"The Kiev Times said a boating accident."

"That's the story Luhansk fed them. Later Mrs. Gubenko learned differently."

"She thought you were there?"

"She asked one night if I was Russian Army. I said not anymore. Years ago I served in Chechnya, but was discharged when my term was up. She couldn't grasp the last part, that I was out of it for good. She wanted me to find out who killed her family."

"You left off going to the soup kitchen at St Basil's, and stopped attending chess night."

"She was embarrassing herself, I couldn't allow it to continue."

"She found you. She asked around, heard you preferred solitude, and that you often camped out in deserted areas."

"You're spinning a tale. After I left St Basils' I never saw her again."

"I think she found you here."

"Never happened."

Injuries consistent with a fall, Ruslan said about Ivana Ivanova, aka Viktoria Gubenko. I play my flashlight in the direction of the marina. The only fall would be down to the marina ice, which is more than sufficient to crack bones, especially if someone struck outcroppings on the way down.

"She was no threat to you, she just wanted answers, but she got under your skin and made you feel you might be a real man after all."

I illuminate his face with my flashlight.

"She made you look at yourself: an unreliable, skulking vagabond. You punished her for it." I point with the flashlight, but he doesn't turn.

"Afterwards you brought her up, laid her under the abutment, lit a bonfire so we'd come and find her. You were here, somewhere in the darkness, watching to make sure she was found."

He's not denying anything so I keep going.

"When you came for your boots you recognized me, and tonight there's another bonfire. Why?"

He's not going to answer any of this. I think when he saw me he remembered Viktoria, and the bonfire is a memorial. The anniversary of a killing. It's also possible he had genuine feelings for her, which wouldn't be inconsistent with murder.

"Put your hands above your head," I tell him.

"You promised you wouldn't arrest me."

"Not for killing Viktoria, but you're good for arson and trespass."

In the end I call for assistance, because he won't comply. He won't run from a lady cop either, his pride won't permit. Two squad cars arrive, and they put him face down and cuff him, and take him away.

Before they do I get a good look at his documents.

The next morning, I learn that Rostik Zemskova is wanted in Chechnya for raping the virgin cousin of an army commander there. Rostik can cut a plea for the murder of Viktoria, or get sent back to face life in a Chechen prison.

His choice, I really don't care.

****

I'm downstairs helping Anna clean her stove, when the door buzzes; Anna opens and signs for a delivery. It's my bathing suit and I dash upstairs to try it on. When I take it out of the package it looks nothing like the promo, it's been fabricated somewhere in Asia, it's paper thin and vaguely sticky, and smells of petroleum. It's also too small, and parts of me that are usually modestly concealed are slipping sideways. I hear Anna coming up and I snatch a blanket from the bed.

My sister frowns. "Let me see."

Anna is a naturally malicious individual, but just now she's pretending she's an actual adult, so I do the reveal.

"It's fine," says Anna.

"Really?"

"You're too self-conscious, Katya, you have a perfectly acceptable body. You should wear it."

Did I misjudge? My sister has made kind remarks and made me feel better.

Anna exits and closes the door, but I soon hear something on the stair. I open the door and find her slumped on a step, cupping a hand over her mouth as she stifles chortles. When she sees me she jumps up guiltily and dashes for safety.

I return to the mirror. The bathing suit reminds me of camouflage-patterned duct tape. Someone made it with a stapler and sweatshop floor scraps, and shipped it as a joke.

***

A picture of myself created by my three-year-old nephew Klem has been scotched to my fridge for two days, because when I first saw it I had some sort of subconscious epiphany, which I'm now trying to winkle out. It won't winkle. All I get is -*it doesn't look like me, but it is.*

Now I frown at the picture again, as my cat Masha sprawls atop my knees, her eyes closed, purring obnoxiously loud. I look at the scrawled colored pencil picture of me, and back at Masha, and I notice the same sort of winged mouth. Something stirs in the murky recesses of my skull, and I have a flashback. I'm sitting in Galina Klepikov's morning room, as I question Senora Saenz about scratches on

Galina's hands. From my vantage point I can see through the French doors into the main dining room, where vases and figurines line a window shelf.

Everything shifts, tumbles, rearranges, falls into place.

I'm so excited I nearly jump up, but fortunately for Masha, I keep my cool. The epiphany wasn't that *the picture doesn't look like me, but it is*. It was even simpler.

It looks like someone's picture.

The bruise on Galina Klepikov's chest, revealed in the autopsy photo, is someone's portrait. And I know whose.

****

My first impulse is to phone detectives Ivan and Bumchik, but I restrain myself. They'll think I'm tweaking on Revo, and I wouldn't blame them. Instead I call Ruslan Omelechko and ask him if he's free. His nose is still out of joint, and he answers a bit stiffly, no he's not, not at the moment. I ignore this and tell him to bring a full size copy of Galina Klepikov's chest autopsy photo to Carbur's Antique shop on Andrew's Descent, as quickly as possible.

I climb into the Volga, head for downtown. In Carbur's I find what I'm looking for in a window display, it's a dull old relic from the soviet days, but there are Ukrainians who cherish this sort of thing, if you can believe, and the value can be prohibitive, which is why I'm not buying. I ask the girl if she'll remove it from the window so I can inspect it, and she places it on the counter with a slight effort. I heft it.

"Wow," I say.

"Filled with lead," she explains.

I give it a try. Ten kilos, easy.

I need to stall for Ruslan, so I tell her I couldn't be more delighted, but I'm going to browse some more.

I browse for half an hour. No Ruslan. The salesgirl is sending me looks and I also need to use a bathroom. Just before I give up hope, Ruslan appears, looking utterly calm, and nicely dressed for the season with a green muffler.

"You took your time," I snap at him.

He unfurls a large autopsy photo. There's no face, only the mammoth silicone-engorged breasts, and between them, the bruises that everyone, including me, thought were made by a fist.

"Hold it up here," I say, pointing to the counter, and then, "Rotate it a few degrees east."

"See?"

He looks at it doubtfully, and then really scrutinizes, and afterwards emits an overused profanity.

"That's the nose, where the skin broke," I say. "Those indented lines above are the brow."

"The winged part beneath - that's the moustache," he continues.

I touch a cleft circle at the bottom. "Chinbone."

We look at each other, then he gravely rolls up the photo.

Galina Klepikov has a portrait of Josef Stalin between her breasts. Or rather, someone hurled a bust of Stalin at her, causing a heart attack. I glimpsed another bust of Stalin in the dining room at Galina Klepikov's house, and it lodged in a corner of my memory because regular people don't keep mementoes of the communist years.

The sales girl is wrapping up the bust, and waiting for a credit card. Instead I call Detectives Ivan and Bumchik. Predictably I'm met with skepticism, but I put Ruslan on briefly to verify.

Ruslan hands back the phone and Bumchik asks rhetorically, "Which of them threw it?"

I remember my dad saying that people fundamentally resent getting advice, and I answer, "The one she loved the most."

The bust of Josef Stalin is more than I can afford, but Uncle Joe and I have made a connection, so I pay without complaint. After that I take Ruslan for dinner, which goes off pretty well, and after that I call Anna to tell her to feed my cat, I won't be home tonight.

***

It's New Year's Day, and the Dneiper isn't frozen; everyone faults global warming. There's a pitiful fringe of ice along the banks, and to call it disastrous is too kind. There's supposed to be a large rectangle cut out of deep winter ice, with steam rising out of black water, and lots of drama and manliness when the guys jump in.

Today is like April in Sevastopol, we're only lacking tulips.

It's been decided we're to dive off a quay, and swim back and climb cement steps where warm towels and hot drinks are waiting. There's a motor launch purring twenty meters out, in case someone seizes up in the water, and a crew from TRU-Vision is filming.

Our very hirsute Commander Shulikov goes first, the commander could work at a car wash, he's a walking bottlebrush. His wife and children stand on the quay, the smallest in a penguin costume. All cheer loudly when Papa comes out of the water and shakes like a dog. Handsome Detective Sanya Zubov disrobes next and he's everything I'd imagined, and my libido is snapping pics for later perusal.

I'm fifth, after Sergeant Dasha, who's the only other female Penguin. I unzip my parka and kick off my boots and pretend I'm not wearing a bathing suit intended for a fourteen-year-old. Anna and her husband, my nieces and nephews, my brother Slava, and my parents and my brother-in-law Ilya's parents, all clap and yowl.

I'm suddenly frightened. I jump without a proper inhalation, down into silt-filled water, the shock of it is unbelievable, I thrash with leaden limbs toward the cement steps, and nearly fall as I climb out. I'm saved from tottering over by Ruslan Omelechko, my medical examiner's intern, and he says. "You did great, now let's get you somewhere warm."

He means his apartment. I make excuses to my sister Anna, and promise I'll be home in time for tarts and pudding, but I have something to take care of first.

Anna relays this to the relatives, who reject it outright. My personal happiness means nothing to my family, and my independence is a delusion. Ruslan and I are hauled back to Anna's place, where we are granted no privacy, and instead endure harassing questions about our relationship, as well as food cooked by two babushkas with lengthy experience in holiday fare, especially desserts.

While the children play with new toys, I cap off the story of Galina Klepikov's murder. Ukrainians don't confess to cops, and rarely rat each other out, but the Sanchez's aren't citizens, and they prove loquacious as they face criminal charges.

Galina's brother Vitaly never gave up smoking, even after he was wheeling an oxygen tank around the mansion. Oxygen tanks plus cigarettes are a perilous combination, and the problem was compounded because Galina loved her big country house as much as she loved Vitaly, but maybe just a little bit more.

I pause in my narration to glance over the table and my mother hurriedly passes me what remains of the buckwheat salad. "Go on, dear."

So Galina threatened to throw Vitaly out, and after a vicious and lengthy argument he mustered the strength to lob Uncle Joe at her. Galina didn't succumb at once, according to Señora Saenz, but shortly after the incident she complained of shortness of breath, retired to her bedroom, and didn't come out.

The other three colluded to get rid of the body by pinning the death on the Trans-Ukraine trucking company, which was carrying on a public spat with Galina over her support of strikers. The caretaker drove Galina's body to Kiev, with Señora Sanchez following in her car. Señor Sanchez had intended to place the body on a loading platform, but instead decided to get creative, and hanged her from the gantry crane. Later he parked the car at Galina's apartment, where his wife collected him.

Galina's orange wig was found snarled up in the tire jack in the trunk of his car.

Klem approaches his father with the remote for the mechanical dinosaur I've given him, and Illya rises to help. The spell of a murder tale is broken; a festive spirit swiftly reasserts and smiles break out, with compliments to the cooks for an exceptional meal. The children chatter and exclaim in the nearby room, the decorations sparkle, and a syrupy carol plays on the radio. In the midst of this tender bonding of loved ones my father is moved to speak.

"The killer is always a family member," says my dad. He's smiling, but his eyes dart speculatively over our faces.

CHAPTER THREE – TANNERY QUAY

-A CONSTABLE KATYA INVESTIGATION-

In every family there's a favorite child, and in mine it's my brother Slava. He's the youngest at age 22, and no one is more pampered, or has suffered more well-intentioned meddling. My sister Anna and I are conspiring to find him a suitable girlfriend, while nudging him away from his current interest, who's urging him to move to Belarus.

We are making kvass and strategizing, while the children nap.

I glance up at the TV screen, as Anna's cooking show is interrupted by a bulletin. Three boys have gone missing; they left their homes yesterday morning, and now thirty hours later the families are in panic mode. A ten-year-old and a thirteen-year-old are brothers, a third boy is a schoolmate. Authorities have ruled out a train excursion after checking station surveillance cams on both sides of the river. Photos of the boys fill the TV screen.

Anna is digging fingertips into her cheek. The boys' names are Misha, Turik, and Vladek.

Our plans for Slava's love life are shelved.

***

When I clock in for the night shift, I'm greeted by a somber mood at headquarters. Everyone on Patrol is given a flyer with photos of the boys, along with a briefing on what's been learned of their plans the day they vanished. "You are not part of a search effort, but I want you in the loop," says Sergeant Dasha. It's already been established that the three deceived their parents: they weren't heading for a football match as they claimed, but instead intended to climb a transmission tower where they would text video of their adventure to friends.

So far, no classmate has come forward with a video, nor has a search of likely towers turned up any clues. Or bodies.

Sergeant Dasha wraps up. "If they were planning to explore the urban landscape, they may have trapped themselves in a derelict building. If you think of something, let me know and I'll relay to the search teams."

The only other idea I have is that the boys are dead, but my hunches have a spotty track record, and I keep my mouth shut.

At midnight I swing down and park near the ferries, and dine on soup and chips. It's May, the air is mild, a garbage truck is making pickups and sea gulls are fighting over spills. It's business as usual, and little by little I grow more optimistic about the missing boys. It's possible they've run away because they're bored with school and boxed-in at home, and tonight they're sleeping rough. In a day or two they'll realize how cozy they had it at mom and dad's, and turn up unharmed.

***

It's now Monday, the morning is clear after two days of cold drizzle, and I have the day free. I phone my brother Slava but don't get an answer. Soon after, my mother calls from Boryspil needing to know where she can buy a memory card for her camera. I give her the name of an electronics store. Next she complains that she's called Slava repeatedly the previous day without an answer, which I suspect is the real reason she's calling me. I advise her to phone Anna, whose tracking system for family members rivals a computer model for the weather. My mother, a graphic arts teacher, says she's late for class, and rings off.

I drive to HQ and ask Sergeant Dasha about volunteering for one of the search teams for the boys, and she tells me if I really want to help I can answer phones; there are tips coming in from as far away as Kharkov and her people can't cope.

She steers me into the briefing room, which is now a call center. The map on the corkboard is a startled hedgehog of stick pins, and across it Kiev sprawls, with hectares of parks, green spaces, and undeveloped swaths overgrown with brush. It's a formidable search area.

"Anything promising?" I ask the Sergeant.

For a moment her guard drops and she seems overwhelmed. "We won't know unless we check them out," she replies vaguely, reaching for a ringing phone.

Constable Gladkov tells me he's gotten a tip from Warsaw, Poland. Evidently the kids have turned up for Polish comic-con, but Mister Gladkov isn't buying it.

"What's your craziest?" I ask, making conversation.

"Take your pick." He digs through a pad, but his phone rings.

****

I take a call from a man who asks why the kids weren't in school on Saturday, and I tell him not every school is open Saturday anymore, and he says that's the problem, isn't it?

The immediate problem is that he's wasting our time, but I say thank you for calling.

In my second hour I get my first drunk. Several days ago she picked up four or five young people, one of which may have been a girl, at an Okko gas station, and dropped them off at Tannery Quay. She's not sure of the day, but it was definitely last week.

"Describe the boys, please."

"Juveniles," she says. "One of them was mouthy. He said I needed driving lessons."

Clothing? Age? Height?

She couldn't determine any of this, because they were wearing baseball caps, and that was all she noticed. "What sort of baseball caps?"

"The ones they wear backwards."

"Did they give a reason for visiting Tannery Quay?"

There's a long silence and I repeat the question.

"They wanted to see a mermaid," she answers, and when I don't react, she breaks into hoarse cackles.

I hang up and ask Constable Gladkov if he's familiar with an urban legend regarding a mermaid at Tannery Quay. He isn't. He confesses he's never heard of Tannery Quay either.

I have. In high school I went pike fishing there with my first boyfriend, Vova Kovacs, only I didn't hook any fish. Not from the river, anyway.

I decide to drive down in the Volga. Like Sergeant Dasha said, we won't know if the tips are worthwhile if we don't check them out. I tell Constable Gladkov my plan before heading to the parking lot.

Forty klicks south of Kiev lies the decaying hamlet of Tannery Quay, hidden in the birch scrub lining the river. You can drive past on P 19 and miss it altogether.

There's one street, the houses are from a couple of centuries ago, and so are the stacks of uncollected garbage. I breeze through town in the direction of the river.

A dozen boats are moored at the edge of a reed marsh, with a channel cleared to the river. Two arms of a rickety walkway hold four rows of watercraft, although several of the berths are vacant. There are two fiberglass boats with big Suzuki engines, and a half dozen battered wooden punts with oars and trolling motors, and a several other fishing boats of intermediate status.

It doesn't look right; it's not the Tannery Quay I remember when I came here with Vova Kovacks when I was fifteen. That day remains blurry, I recall searching for birds' nests among the bulrushes, and I remember Vova's teeth scraping against mine before we both opened our mouths.

***

I backtrack up a potholed asphalt ramp, rise on tiptoe to call over a slatted blue fence. A young fellow emerges and lets me in, and I identify myself, and ask how he's doing. He tells me he's readying the place for summer use. Did he see kids at the dock on Saturday? No, miss. Didn't hear unusual noise? No, miss. Did any of his neighbors report vandalized property?

I return to the river bank. I notice a preserves jar of pale green glass partially imbedded in shore mud; I retrieve it and rinse it, and kneel precariously on wobbling stones to fill it among the reeds. I don't get what I'm trying for until several scoops later, but finally I'm satisfied. My sneakers are slick with mud in spite of taking care, and I spend another five minutes wiping them.

I stop at the grocer's, a cement bunker with barred windows. There's a real steal on frozen catfish, but I settle for soda and chips, and ask if a group of school kids stopped in on Saturday. The cashier says she doesn't believe so, she'd know because she had the morning shift. Next I ask what happened to the tannery at Tannery Quay. The girl yells in back and a gentleman with fluffy white hair emerges to give me a history lesson. The Tannery was moved to Kiev in 1960, and many of the towns' residents followed.

"You stayed."

"I'd had my fill of it," he tells me. "In those days it wasn't done by machines, with the fellows giving a poke and a nudge, like now. It was slave labor, and a filthy business."

I head back into Kiev. I feel ambiguous about wasting time on a fruitless excursion instead of manning the police hotline, but it's my day off and the weather's been yummy.

At home I detour on my way upstairs to collect my cat Masha, and say hello to my niece and nephews. I have golden minnows from among the river reeds at Tannery Quay, darting in a green glass jar. I warn the kids to keep it out of Masha's reach.

"Did Mom call?" I ask my sister.

"No, what's going on?"

"We can't reach Slava."

Anna reaches for her phone and presses a number. She listens for half a minute, then turns to me. "Voicemail."

"He's busy at work," I speculate. Anna rolls her eyes. Slava is a member of a design team at a tech company; the kind that lets you bring your pet gecko, and encourages napping after lunch.

Anna has a more likely explanation. "They're in the early stages," she says, referring to Slava's new girl. She means that during the first days of a new relationship, Slava is often very *busy*. "Give him two more days and he'll pick up his phone," she says.

***

The following afternoon I'm on patrol when Sergeant Dasha calls my mobile. She's taken a call from Tannery Quay for a cop named Katya. I think it's my friend who was renovating his place for summer. The message is that one of his neighbors discovered his boat in the wrong berth. An oar was missing, as well as a six-inch curved fish knife from the tackle box.

I sense the sergeant's antennae are quivering, even if I can't see her. "Is this related to the missing boys, Constable?" she asks.

I'm picturing the boat landing. I have a sudden vision of three boys stealing a punt to go fishing.

I tell her one of my callers drove a group of boys to Tannery Quay, but the woman was fuzzy on details. I explain that I swung by and talked to the locals, but came away empty handed.

"If someone's tampered with a boat, it could be them," I say.

"How sure are you?"

"I'm not sure, but I have a bad feeling," I reply.

"Constable Kondrashov, should I look into this?"

I deflect. "You'll need a diving team, and a second team to sweep the shore line."

I think she's going to give it a pass, then she tells me to come in. "You're going with them, Constable."

****

The volume of man power and emergency vehicles that converges on the town boat landing has me worried that I've led everyone on a wild goose chase, but it's a risk I can live with.

The dive team decides to start at the landing and work downstream.

I'm with a shore team of three, which includes Sergeant Dasha and Constable Gladkov, besides myself. We wait as forensics examines the misplaced punt. The owner claims he uses it infrequently and no one else has his say-so to borrow. There's blood on the floor of the boat, and although it's likely old fish blood, samples are swabbed. The remaining oar is bagged for fingerprints, as well as a cigarette packet and an empty bottle of Ron Kola, which the owner denies are his.

I lead the sergeant and Mister Gladkov upstream, because I've remembered the quay part of Tannery Quay. There's a narrow footpath, partially obscured by rampant spring growth of weeds and saplings. A kilometer further on we find the old quay.

We stand on the stone quayside, and swipe away midges. The old shipping channel was dug deep, the water is free of rushes, and naked pilings extend toward a gap between two small islands. Beyond is the open river. From here the hides came in, and leather was shipped out.

This is also where Vova and I cast our lines.

"There's narrow gauge rail," says Gladkov. He points to rails that lead away from the river into dense trees, and we follow. We climb a slope though brush and the occasional litter of discarded household trash. Where the brush finally clears there are eight or ten stone buildings, roof timbers exposed, wild grape curling across the grey walls.

"The tannery!" exclaims sergeant Dasha.   I'm not sure if she's astonished, or just gasping for breath from the exercise.

We check the buildings one by one until Gladkov calls out. "Someone's in this one."

We stand outside a window frame and peer in. A small figure is stretched in the rubble and flies swarm around him.

I give Sergeant my arm and she maneuvers through the window. She kneels beside the figure and checks for signs of life.

"He's still with us," she announces. Gladkov is already on his phone. I climb inside.

The boy's pant leg is torn; his leg is purple-black and massively swollen. A gash across his calf oozes pink slime. He breathes with shallow, rasping attempts.

"He's pretty far gone," says Sergeant.   "Sepsis shock and dehydration."

"I'm calling the dive teams," I tell her. "If he swam ashore nearby, then whatever happened took place upstream from the landing."

Sergeant shrugs out of her backpack and removes a bottled water, puts it to the boy's lips. I'm thinking it's the youngest, the ten-year-old.

He drinks, and whispers.

"Did you catch that?" I ask, as I wait for the divers to respond.

"*Rusalka*," says Sergeant Dasha. "He said 'rusalka.'"

****

It's midnight before the teams return to the town landing, electric torchlight wavering over the river. They have the bodies of the two older boys, extricated from among the reeds. By now we've learned that the younger, whom we located at the old tannery, has died on the way to the hospital.

There are stoic faces among the divers, but I know everyone prayed for a better ending, and the faces conceal grief.

Finally, Mister Gladkov voices what no one has thought to ask. If the boys borrowed the boat with the missing knife and oar, who returned it?

****

I go to Slava's apartment, knock, use my key. I step inside and immediately have the sense of a space that's been deserted; lingering odors have faded, heat signatures have gone cold, and there's that certain kind of stillness that settles in after protracted abandonment.

A post-it on a cupboard door reads: "At any moment in an ongoing process, there's completion."

Words to die by, I murmur to myself. But this is Slava, and I try to un-think what's just come to mind.

A bit guiltily I push open his bedroom door. There are tidy stacks of books along the walls and at the foot of the bed. I know Slava reads books, but I assumed like a normal person, one or two a year.

The bed is unmade, a pink e-cigarette and charger occupy a bedside table.

I select a book at random, it's by Schopenhauer and there's a note inside the cover in my mother's hand, recommending passages.

A few books later I find a book of Ivan Franko's poetry inscribed by my father! At this point my jaw is on the floor. Who are we kidding here? This is carefree Slava!

I count over thirty books from my parents before I stop looking, because I'm thinking about my parents' gifts to me. (New Years' I asked jokingly for McDonald's gift certificates, and I'm still eating caramel parfaits).

We all indulge Slava, but I suddenly feel as if my parents *value* me less. I'm on the verge of a monumental sulk and I leave in a hurry.

In the street I call his work number and am told that Slava is on leave, and has been for a week.

I'm now beyond alarmed. I'm even frightened to tell Anna.

****

That night I research *mermaid at Tannery Quay*. There's nothing in the mainstream news. I find a blurred photo of a female swimmer on Instagram, another on Tumblr, both purported to be sightings on the Dneiper.

It's an internet rumor.

I search google images, find the same blurred photo with a website link, which turns out to be NewsNow, a UK sports magazine, and the article details the tribulations of a Ukrainian female swimmer. In 1972 she was sanctioned by the IOC and stripped of a medal in the 25-kilometer open water race. Reason given –doping. The swimmer's name was Jana Stepanyuk, and the photo is from a year ago, when Jana attempted unsuccessfully to swim the English Channel.

***

I make a second trip to Slava's apartment with the intention of leaving a note.

While my key is still in the lock the door is jerked open from within. The girl in Slava's apartment appears as disconcerted as I.

She squeaks. "I thought it was…"

"I'm Katya."

She's really pretty. She has an eyebrow piercing with three silvery beads, and a spider web tattoo encircles her neck. Her name is Iryna, and she's picking up clothing. Slava's been staying at her place.

"Why isn't he at work?"

She's been told by Slava not to say.

"I'm seconds away from reporting a missing person," I warn.

She screws up her face, wracked by indecision, but not for long. Slava's gone for a walk to Trukhaniv Island.

I park my car near the footbridge.

I find him midpoint on Park Bridge, not bright Slava, but new, haunted Slava. By now I realize how slender my connection to my brother has become. We're strangers, and I'm not certain who's at fault.

He doesn't notice me until I'm squarely in front of him, glaring accusingly. He glares back. "Go away, Katya. Mind your own business."

He may as well have struck me. I pivot to the railing and the river, while he strides toward downtown. I feel as though Slava's been physically gouged from my body, and my world is collapsing around a vile and painful vacuum. I don't believe anything could be worse.

I hear his voice behind me.

"Katya, listen. I have cancer."

****

We find a café and talk. Slava won't endure chemo, he'd rather jump off a bridge.

Nor does he want his life to end, but he struggles to envision a future. He laughs bitterly. "It's over, I'm a total failure."

I don't attempt to offer advice, nor do I give credence to his threat to hurt himself. Now that I know what's going on, it seems to me that he's infinitely safer. I think, *we've got him now, all of us together, and we'll keep harm at bay.*

****

"I've found Slava," I blurt to Anna.

I push her into a chair, and put on water to boil.

I tell my sister what I've learned. "He's in early stages, and success rates for treatment are high."

Anna looks stricken, but also betrayed. This is Slava, who confides everything in her.

"He needed time to figure things out."

"That's what *we're* for," Anna protests.

I open a cupboard and sort through fruity-flowery flavored teabags. Later, we sit and sip, and finally Anna says, "One of us needs to call mom and dad."

"I think that should be Slava," I say, knowing I'll be ignored.

"You're right, of course." She wipes her eyes, and reaches for her phone.

****

I return to Tannery Quay on another morning, about the same time I calculate the boys would have arrived on the day they were attacked, and I'm alone because I haven't shared my whacko hypothesis at HQ. No else suspects that a killer mermaid haunts the Dneiper river.

I'm not at the town landing, instead I sit cross legged under the trees above the old tannery quay, and although I'm not in uniform I've brought a gun. I've since learned that disgraced Olympic swimmer Jana Stepanyuk, now Jana Postol, was living near Lvov until recently, when her husband inherited his mother's house in Ukrainka. Ukrainka, by the way, is just up the road.

I'm alerted by a pheasant, rocketing out of the sedge. I watch Jana Postol approach from the direction of the landing. Without checking her surroundings, she strips off a track suit and stands poised on the quayside, completely nude. She raises her arms to free lank grey tresses from a hairclip.

Rusalka.

I leave the trees and stride downhill, calling out as the woman dives. She strokes steadily toward the opening between the islands. I stop where the narrow gauge ends. I remember the drunken lady who picked up the kids at an Okko gas station, saying one of them was mouthy, mocking her driving skills.

I think the three kids in the stolen punt, drinking Ron Kola and smoking cigarettes, saw an old naked woman swimming in the middle of the Dneiper, and they couldn't resist jeers and catcalls.

Maybe they threw a soda can, or poked her with an oar.

I return to the town landing at a run, commandeer one of the big Suzuki outboards, and head out through the reed channel and swerve upstream. I'm abreast of the twin islands, when I spot her gliding over sun spangled water. I pull up and cut her off.

She rears out of the water like a dolphin, and grips the gunwale.

"I'm here to ask a few questions, Jana." I keep my hand on the tiller in case she peels away.

"You had a run-in with three kids in a fishing boat," I say, not making it a question.

"Who the devil are you?"

"Constable Kondrashov, Kiev Patrol Unit."

She snorts, falls back and swims away. I rotate the throttle and cut her off again.

This time she emerges near the stern and her hand gropes over the engine mount. "You need to move away from me, miss," she tells me.

She grabs for my arm, but I'm no twelve-year-old, and I haul her halfway out of the water and jam a gun to her forehead.

Suddenly she screams. Her fury is primal and instinctive, it's the thrashing of a big pike on a stainless steel hook.

"You don't know! You don't know!"

She twists free and sinks down, down, and she's gone, until I see her swimming well beyond my bow, and more than a meter below the surface. She's moving preternaturally swiftly, as if she had fins. About ten meters out she surfaces, only to grab a lungful and submerge again. I wait with the motor idling, wondering what to do next, convinced there'll be more victims if she's not stopped.

I scan the river, shaking with nerves. I feel I've let a big one get away, but in the end reasonable doubt sneaks in; there's nothing linking Jana Postol to a crime. I can only hope she drowns.

She reappears midstream, where the current carries her, and the spring sun glints on her shimmering skin.

CHAPTER FOUR – BLOOD CHRISTENING
A CONSTABLE KATYA INVESTIGATION

PART I – Church Massacre

I leave the Liberty Café, black tea sloshing in a cup, and slip into Dubke Park, where I cut across a cobbled path imbedded with tram rails, and pass beneath the incurious gaze of our city founders. I look for the red squirrels but don't see them. Near the exit, smoke from a trash barrel infuses the air with a cocktail of burning plastic, rotting food, and a bum's old socks, and it stinks like the end of the world.

I'm a road cop, on scene to keep traffic flowing during Kutsenko & Kasko's razing of Dubke Park. I reach my car and have a quick breakfast of donuts and tea, and then shift into low for a recon of the portable chain link along Tolstoi St. At the west entrance I pass elderly retirees and a half dozen moms with strollers, doubtless hoping their voices will be heeded and their park will be spared. I reverse onto the sidewalk, kill the engine, and for a few seconds I entertain an unexpected thought. What would it *really* take to save Dubke Park?

I know what *won't* work. Holding up a placard with crayoned letters.

Heavy machinery approaches, and sparrows on the cobbled path take flight. A transmission van from TRU-Vision TV rolls past, just ahead of Kutsenko & Kasko's caravan of backhoes and bulldozers, and the cluster of protestors brandish their cardboard signs.

So long, Dubke Park.

***

At 12:30 I'm at Domashnya Kyhnya for an order of stuffed peppers, when I answer a radio call.

"Constable Kondrashov, how close are you to St. Ignatius?"

"Five minutes."

"They need a female officer on scene."

I forget about lunch, flick on the siren and race down Peremohy to Zhylianska, and I'm at St. Ignatius in three minutes. Four squad cars and Commander Shulikov's SUV are skewed haphazardly under the horse chestnuts and I can hear a discordant orchestra of sirens in the distance.

I'm stopped at the door by an officer I don't recognize. "I was sent by dispatch," I explain.

"Wait here."

He steps back, and no I don't wait there, I slip inside where a second officer raises his arm like a toll boom. I don't know this one either. The first officer passes into the nave and I glimpse a wedge of iconostasis before the door swings shut.

The first officer reemerges, followed by Commander Shulikov bearing an infant in a white dress, with a head band topped by a white fabric rose.

"Oh, it's you, Miss Kondrashov. Good." He hands the baby to me. "Take the child to HQ and give Family Services a heads-up."

"Name? Relatives?"

"We're sorting it out." He orders the constable, whose name turns out to be Skakun, to assist me. "Miss Kondrashov will need the child's car seat. Here's hoping the parents didn't think to lock up."

The commander reenters the nave. I follow Mr. Skakun down the steps, in time to avoid a rush of emergency personnel toward the doors. Behind the church, we locate a grey Mazda with a car seat, which Constable Skakun slides out of its bars, and I walk him through seatbelt installation in my patrol car, while I cradle the sleeping baby. She has a woody smell, and after attending the christenings of my sister's kids, I know this fragrance to be myrrh.

By now I've figured out that the little girl's mom and dad haven't surrendered her voluntarily.

"How bad is it?" I ask the constable.

"All victims deceased," he tells me. He gives the kiddy seat an experimental tug. "Except for the priest."

****

Of course I don't take the baby to HQ, I shoot over to my sister Anna's, who's en route to the neighborhood playground with my niece and two nephews.

"I have a situation," I tell her, unstrapping my passenger.

Anna sees the baby, and since she can't resist, she says, "This is so sudden, Katya. Do I know the daddy?"

I say bring the kids back inside, and she does what I tell her, because she wants to hear details. In the kitchen I perch on a munchkin stool and Anna and her offspring surround me.

 "She was being christened, I'm guessing the parents are dead or injured."

"Блин!" My sister lets loose with her favorite expletive. She drops onto a chair, mouth gaping, tears welling.

"What's her name?"

"We don't know yet."

She snuffles and digs for a tissue, then squints at the baby. "Katya!" She gingerly removes the head band, and holds it up, and I make out tiny flecks of blood on the white satin rose. More blood speckles the child's head.

"That's evidence," I say.

Anna takes the baby from me. "Hand me a tissue," she snaps.

As she cleans the blood the baby wakes. Her grey eyes are solemn, her little brows black and prominent. She looks wise, but don't we all, until we learn how things work.

"Heat a bottle, would you?" Anna hoists the infant, carries her into the kids' bedroom, and the children scramble after their mama like ducklings.

She's back in five, frowning at a saucepan I've placed on the stove. "Were you born in the stone age?"

She opens the microwave and scoots the formula inside.

"Sorry about interrupting play time," I say.

"I'll ask Lydia to take the kids." She means her mother-in-law. "So what else do you know?"

"Just speculation."

"I enjoy speculation," says my sister.

****

I spend the afternoon at Dubke park. Now and then I check news on my phone - as many as seven are dead at St Ignatius Cathedral, multiple gunmen being sought.

There are more victims at Dubke park- all red squirrels- squashed in the street as they fled, their homes dismantled limb by limb, and the stumps bulldozed and hauled away. A chainsaw biting into a tree has the sensory appeal of a raging toothache, and by sundown I'm ready for a vodka anesthetic.

The crowd swells as people leave work, and they're in a restless mood. The action shifts when the crane arrives that's going to remove the statues of Kyi, Shchek, and Khoryv. Tru-Vision cameras swiftly reposition, because when it comes to patriotic symbols no one chokes up faster than a Ukrainian. People who don't give a twig about oak trees lose their cool when city founders are carted away.

A small army of black-suited Kutsenko & Kasko security people attempts to block the camera crew, but they falter when a male reporter exits a Tru-Vision van and strides their way. It's Dimitri Nikolaychuk, Tru-Vision heart-throb reporter, former football player for Dynamos.

There's a short confab, then cameras are allowed to film as the three brothers are hoisted onto a flatbed and secured. Outbursts erupt at this point and the street is suddenly clogged. I'm screaming at people and writing tickets at the same time.

The flatbed pulls away, the truck cab is pelted by stones, and then it's out of control and the black uniforms from Kutsenko are running.

I'm running too and radioing for an ambulance because I can see Kutsenko security personnel are pounding the stuffing out of someone. I push my way through a chaotic throng of demonstrators, and discover an old woman in a bright blue coat and blue knit cap on the ground, bleeding from the mouth. The security goons give ground at the sight of a real uniform, even if it's only a lady patrol cop.

I kneel and assure the woman help is coming, although I'm not sure she's conscious. Others quickly act to make her more comfortable. When she comes around she's stoic. "I hit one with an oak branch," she tells me. It's ten minutes before the stretcher arrives, medics think she has fractured ribs and a broken arm, a possible concussion. Two squad cars roll up; I point them toward the security teams.

I return to my car in the light of street lamps, just in time to collide with TV reporter Dimitri Nikolaychuk.

"Nice work," he says.

"Thanks." I attempt to open my door, but he's not budging.

"Weren't you at the New Year's Penguin Swim for disabled cops?" he asks.

I was wearing a bathing suit made of glue and shoe laces, so I'm not surprised he remembers, and I'm expecting him to make a crack.

Only he doesn't. Instead he asks what I think of the changes at Dubke park.

"I think people hate seeing their neighborhood trashed by autocrats and scoundrels."

He gives me a measuring look. "Is it Tanya? Katya?"

"It's Constable Kondrashov," I answer.

"Miss Kondrashov, would you mind coming over to the cameras and sharing your thoughts?"

"Can't. I work for the city, and the developer has city permits." This sounds self important even to me, but Dimitri nods.

"Fair enough." He reaches to shake my hand, which goes well except I nearly grab for my gun in reflex. "Nice meeting you," he says.

The handshake makes me aware of his height and lean striker's build in an immediate way.

"I saw you leaving St Ignatius with a baby," he tells me. "I'm wondering if you can tell me what it was like inside."

Now I see what this is about.

"I'd lose my job if I did," I answer.

This time I open my door hard enough to crack him across the knees.

****

When I clock out I'm feeling dirty and tired. I run into my friend Detective Volodney, who's working late on the christening case.

"Any updates?" I ask.

"We're thinking traditional deer hunting rifles," he tells me.

"How many shooters?"

"Definitely more than one."

I learn that the priest who survived was shot through the collarbone and neck, and hasn't provided a description of the assassins. An elderly aunt also survives, initially believed dead. She suffered a shattered leg, which was amputated in surgery earlier this afternoon.

The victims include the young parents, both sets of grandparents, and a younger sister of the mother. I scan Volodney's slide show of crime scene photographs. The dead lie in a huddled group, as if no one thought to run. The baptismal font has a hole in it.

"Keep this to yourself?"

"Sure."

"One of the grandfathers was a Golden Eagle."

Golden Eagles, the Berkut, were the riot police who killed more than a hundred civilians in Independence Square during the Maidan uprising. I immediately think what any Ukrainian would.

 "That's motive."

Volodney smiles with one side of his mouth. "Motive for a thousand suspects, but maybe someone in particular made recent threats."

****

When I arrive home Anna's family is tucked in for the night. I burgle her fridge, removing boiled eggs, radishes, rye, mayo. I bring everything upstairs. My cat Masha is a lump under the bedding, and I peel back the cover as she stretches. I press a morsel of egg against her nose, thinking what a good provider I am.

PART II – The Mouflon Gun Club

As I leave Sergeant Dasha's morning briefing, Sanya Zubov strides past me in the opposite direction. He doesn't acknowledge me, but my feelings aren't hurt because I'm devoid of pride when my libido is smitten. I spin on my heel and tag along.

Two months ago Sanya was drafted by a task force investigating the Odessa mafia, even though the Odessa mafia is not a problem for people who don't hire sex workers, gamble, or buy goods on the black market. The mafia is mostly a problem for members of parliament, who need to replace revenues they've diverted to bank accounts in Panama.

Handsome Sanya comes to a stop before his former partner's desk.

"Look what the dog barfed up," says Volodney.

"Touchy," Sanya observes. "Jealous of a co-worker's salary hike, I'm guessing. Did you hear I get bonus vacation days?"

Volodney pretends this is beneath him, instead he asks, "Miss Kondrashov, is there a reason you're lurking?"

I can feel the blood leaving my face, it must be obvious that I'm a sicko stalker.

"Curiosity, Mr. Volodney," I lie. "I happened to notice Mr. Zubov come in, and assumed he had information on the St Ignatius case."

At this juncture I'm thinking Sanya will turn in my direction, and I'll feel the gaze of those astonishing gray eyes, like a car heater blasting warm air on a winter morn. Instead he pulls a no-brand, no-tax-stamp, pack of smokes from an inner pocket and drops it next to Mister Volodney's plum platz.

"Product of Uzbekistan," says Zubov. "Discovered in a raid on a warehouse owned by Sergei Litvak."

"*My* Sergei Litvak?"

Sergei Litvak is Ina's father, the young man murdered at the christening. Mister Zubov now informs us that Litvak was part of a smuggling ring bringing cigarettes from Tashkent, and bypassing the Odessa mafia, which means Litvak could have been the target of the St Ignatius attack.

"Doesn't this muddy the water?" I blurt.

"The simplest answer is usually the correct one, Miss Kondrashov." Volodney claps Sanya Zubov on the back, and steers him toward the door. I overhear something about an early beer. I'm hoping to get invited, but this is Katya Kondrashov's life, and miracles are scarce.

I'd also hoped to point out that the Odessa mafia isn't known for its use of deer rifles.

****

Family Services has lodged a complaint against yours truly, Miss Katya Kondrashov, stopping short of kidnapping charges. All will be forgiven if an infant I've abducted, Irina Litvak, is turned over to authorities.

Ina has an aunt and uncle in Kharkov, whose fitness as guardians is under review. The uncle was recently released from jail, but I don't know the particulars.

"This can't be it."

I've been deceived into believing I'm bringing Ina to a home-style facility, providing exceptional one-on-one care. I'm expecting tidy walkways bordered by flower beds, instead I find a rusting steel door leading into a damp tunnel, emerging at the bottom of an airshaft, where I pull back a second rusting door. Ina is strapped against Anna's chest, burbling inquisitively.

"I've brought Irina Litvak," I inform the outer office attendant.

The woman is a sour, dour leftover from hammer and sickle days, keen to demonstrate bureaucratic hindrance. She passes me a clipboard and orders me to sign and date each of eight pages, affirming that Ina has been in my care without authorization, that I'm liable for illnesses contracted in the interim, and that I plead no contest to being a reprehensible member of society. Meanwhile the attendant slams back a counter flap and approaches Anna. She extends flabby arms, which my sister doesn't deign to acknowledge.

Anna taught secondary school before she married; she's blind and deaf to screams, tears, wheedling, and most of all, intimidation. She brushes the matron aside and makes a beeline for the nursery.

I follow, thinking the chances of little Ina Litvak ever leaving here are slender, diminishing to nil, even if the unfit relatives in Kharkov sign off on adoption. Ukraine's orphanages have no waiting lists of prospective parents, no lines out the door, few takers. Thirty-five thousand kids wait for a home as our country's economy freefalls down a sinkhole.

Large cribs hold as many as eight, little heads swivel toward the entrance. They know. Barely able to stand, they know their only hope is the door swinging open.

Anna covers Ina's face from this sight, and we leave the way we came. Comrade Clipboard threatens to summon police, and I flash my badge at her.

Anna and I have a spat in the car.

"You can't keep her. She has relatives."

"Go to hell, Katya."

****

Minutes later I'm stifling a yawn in downtown traffic when a female producer from Tru-Vision TV calls for Miss Kondrashov. I say she's not available. Another voice breaks in.

"I need a small favor," says Dimitri Nikolaychuk, TV reporter and one-time Dynamos striker.

"Who did you bribe for my number?" I'm surly because I'm embarrassed that I overreacted at Dubke Park, when I kneecapped him with my car door.

"It's essential I get video of the baby."

"What baby?"

On cue, Ina squalls from the back seat.

"Miss Kondrashov, the citizens of Kiev have a right to be informed."

I hang up. He's pushy and I'm steamed, but at the same time I'm thinking he's not that old. Thirty-two? Thirty-four tops.

"Who was it?" asks my nosy sister.

"Dimitri Nikolaychuk."

Anna rolls her eyes. "I wasn't born yesterday."

Anna thinks everyone on TV is a celeb; they don't ring up while you're waiting in traffic.

****

I wake up humming *"Bride"* by Egor Kreed. My subconscious is hinting that I'm ready for a serious relationship. Woo-hoo. Yay. I put on lipstick in case I meet my future husband today.

Anna's house is straining at the seams; my parents arrived from Boryspil and slept the night on the slide-away. They're here to hold my brother Slava's hand and consult with doctors, after Slava's final radiation session on Monday.

My mother studies her laptop. "They've upgraded the priest's condition," she reports.

"From the christening massacre?" I ask. My mother's mouth twitches. She's the stable and grounded parent, but within her gentle heart smolder red coals of odium toward priests. My father, the paranoid and hostile parent, saves his passion for whatever invades his personal comfort zone.

From his high chair, my nephew Klem is grappling with the lyrics of "Antoshka," a childrens' ditty that points out the wisdom of helping with the potato harvest. His father Ilya coaches him through the first line, *Антошка, Антошка, Пошли копать картошку!* My mother is biting her tongue because Ilya's teaching the song in Russian, and employing bad grammar to boot.

"Didn't you have a Kutsenko in Public Works?" she inquires of my dad. He's spooning up kasha like a starved teen, and she's obliged to reach with a fork and stab him. He grunts, I can't tell whether in affirmation or otherwise, but my mom is satisfied.

"I'm off that detail," I throw out.

"Which detail?" asks my father.

"Traffic cop for Kutsenko & Kasko," I answer.

"What are you on about, Katya?" asks my mom. "Kutsenko is the priest's name."

It slowly sinks in, and I reach for my phone and call Detective Volodney. "Can you get a list of Kutsenko & Kasko owners and partners?" I ask him. "That's the outfit putting up an office tower in Dubke Park."

"I'll get back to you."

When I hang up my mother's eyes sparkle. She thinks she's gotten the priest in trouble.

****

Reverend Kutsenko is the cousin of Vitaly Kutsenko, of Kutsenko & Kasko, and it's unclear whether the Reverend owns a stake in the construction company. Although Detective Volodney has dug this up without asking questions, now that he's turned it over he demands to know my interest. I tell him it's a loose end, not to fret, but I can tell he doesn't believe me.

The elderly woman beaten in the park has been released from the hospital, and I know this because Tru-Vision filmed her homecoming. To their credit, Tru-Vision and Dimitri Nikolaychuk have pointed out that city residents aren't consulted on projects that gobble up green spaces, and have reminded viewers that Kiev was once called "the city in the forest."

I drop by Mrs. Gorodetsky's on my lunch hour. In Dubke Park the backhoes are busy tearing up tree roots, chewing a widening crater where the oaks stood for centuries. The street gutters are lined with this year's crop of acorns, and I stoop to gather a handful and stuff them in my pocket.

Two of Mrs. Gorodetsky's neighbors are watching over her, and I'm welcomed with smiles. Her neighbors have piled food on the kitchen table until it's swaybacked, and I'm reminded how truly awesome Ukrainian women are.

I add a box of chocolates, and ask the patient how she's doing. Mrs. Gorodestsky appears peaked and tired reclining on her sofa, she's mummified in bandaging, one arm's splinted, and I'm informed that the blurred vision and headaches come and go. In a weak voice she praises me as her savior and swears she'd be a goner if I hadn't jumped in when I did. I'm not sure she's wrong.

I drink tea and munch almond cookies, which would be pleasant except for the jackhammers below the window. I've come to see how she's doing, but I also have questions, and I'm debating how to approach a sensitive topic. The topic is that someone enraged by the Dubke Park destruction may have gone to St. Ignatius to kill a priest, and ended up killing an innocent family.

I begin obliquely. I hint that there's a possibility the construction company had someone masquerading as a protestor, identifying the troublemakers. I nod gravely toward Mrs. G. as a prime example of instigator.

"This person might have advocated violence, hoping to attract support."

Blank looks.

"Anyone who seemed out of place at the protest? Someone you hadn't seen in the neighborhood? A houligan?"

More shrugs and blank faces.   Maybe they're just tired of me. I've had my tea, I've been thanked effusively, time for me to go?

Out of the blue, because I can't think of anything else, I ask if there've been problems with other tenants. This time I connect.

Turns out there was a drug addict in apartment 15, a man in his thirties with a young child, who attacked people and robbed them, even mothers with children, and repeated calls to the police were unheeded.

"They wait until someone's been murdered."

Then it was resolved.

"How?"

The artist fellow. The nicest young man, they all agree. At a tenant's meeting three months ago, he promised to deal firmly with the reprobate. He said anything could be accomplished if one had the will.

The next day, *the very next morning*, the drug addict and his little boy were gone.

The artist's name is Anatoly. Everyone calls him Tolya. Last name? Kornelyuk?

He makes robots out of wires. Statues out of computer parts.

I leave thinking I've hit a dead end. I don't recall the last time a sculptor took out a family at a christening with a deer rifle, but it's all I've got. If he ousted the drug addict in Mrs. Gorodetsky's building, it probably involved threats of violence.

I'm not going to knock on his door, I don't have a valid excuse. Instead I call art co-ops and galleries. Everyone's heard of Tolya Kornelyuk, no one's sure where he's exhibiting.

Eventually I get steered to the Gallery of Ukrainian Modernism on Propizna Street.

I swing by the gallery just before closing. It's got a pretentious name for a hole in the wall. Two life-size green people made of computer cables, circuit boards, and mouse clickers pose in a window. They're cleverly made, they're also innocuous and don't appear to be the work of a maniac.

I take out my phone, dial the Gallery, slur my voice. "I have Tolya's... bottle-opener," I giggle.

"You just missed him," says the girl impatiently. "He's gone down the street to the club." She hangs up.

I walk down the street. I don't see a club. Then I do.

It's a gun club.

****

My brother-in-law Illya has a blanket tented over his head, he has the flu, and is inhaling the restorative steam of boiled potatoes. Anna and my mother have taken the children to the park, and I'm feeding Ina. Her breathing is stuffy but Anna claims it's not the flu, just normal baby stuff.

My dad is pretending to read, but he's fidgety and he's glaring my way.

I conclude that he secretly wants to hold the baby, but doesn't want to ask. I hand over Ina and her bottle, along with a fresh diaper in case. My father acts imposed upon, but what else is new? I sprint upstairs, open my laptop on the bed, and as expected, my cat Masha decides the keyboard is the perfect place for a nice lie-down. We negotiate, she settles for the crook of my arm, and I type one-handed the name of the gun club which Anatoly Kornelyuk visited last night.

Here's my train of thought. Anatoly boasted at a tenant meeting that he could get rid of a drug dealer terrorizing his building, so he sees himself as a vigilante. Kornelyuk also visits a gun club, where he has access to hunting rifles, and maybe he had something to do with the massacre at St. Ignatius, where a priest named Kutsenko was connected to the razing of a beloved neighborhood park.

It's meandering, I know. I'm overthinking, I know. Welcome to Katya's brain.

My laptop delivers. The Mouflon Gun Club offers a range of goodies online: binoculars, telescopes, night vision devices, knives, revolvers, Zippos and air guns. I click on SERVICES and find hunting and fishing expeditions, marksmanship training, survivalist courses, home protection/ electronics installation. I'm looking for assassins for hire, but wouldn't you know, they're not listed.

****

Next day on lunch break I stop by the gun club, in uniform, and browse the display case of handguns. Behind the counter a woman is placating someone on the phone, then she steps away and another clerk emerges.

This is Anatoly Kornelyuk, Tolya to his buddies. I've located his photo on the website of The Gallery of Ukrainian Modernism, and now I know his association with the Mouflon Club – he's an employee. Tolya is mid-twenties, sturdily build but on the flabby side, and he possesses two prominent upper incisors. He's been primping; a gelled and coiled forelock resembles a bed spring.

Mr. Kornelyuk asks if he can assist, I pointedly ignore him. Was I interested in anything in particular? "I'll know when I see it," I mutter testily.

Tolya Kornelyuk blinks, stung. Maybe he thinks he's being disrespected for the beaver teeth. I don't disabuse him. I've decided to bully him because I need to know if he's a bully too.

I plant my hands on the glass top counter, and scan the rifles racked behind the counter. It's quite an arsenal. I glance down, and between my hands there's a sign-up sheet scotched to the glass. It's for skeet practice at rustic Linden Tree Farm, which according to the notice is located twenty minutes outside Kiev. An hour long session, advanced students only.

"How much?" I ask, sending him a look of complete scorn. I'm a traffic cop, so I know what it's like to be on the receiving end of contempt. It's annoying, unless you have delicate feelings, in which case it's a stab in the heart.

Anatoly is red faced and shaking as he signs me up for a Saturday afternoon. A few more minutes and I'd have him snarling, but I don't think he's a bully. I peg him as the passive-aggressive type.

I return to work, speculating how beaver-toothed Anatoly persuaded a violent drug addict to bolt from his apartment without notice, overnight, and I'm beginning to wonder why I'm bothering, and exactly who I'm investigating.

I'm losing the thread. How did I wind up paying for skeet classes? Let's see, *the priest's name was Kutsenko, and the Kutsenkos are building offices in Dubke park, and then....*

Hell with it, I'm over it. I'm finished.

Except I'm not. And this is why.

****

I'm lunching on a chicken Caesar roll-up, a Red Bull, and two slices of cheesecake, while parked on the top of a city garage overlooking the ferries. I'm wondering if I can track the drug addict who preyed on Mrs. Gorodetsky's neighbors. I enter the address of the apartment building into the HQ data base, specify drug activity, and come up with the name Kiril Akhmentov. Five reports of assault, two arrests, suspect released both times when witnesses failed to show. This is not atypical. I discover a third complaint erroneously referred to Narcotics without follow-up, probably because the narcotics division doesn't handle muggings for drug money.

I can see why it seemed to old Mrs. Gorodetsky and her pals that the police ignored them.

I search for a current address, and come up empty. Recent contact with law enforcement? Nope. There was a child staying with him, according to the ladies, so there might be a record with Family Services, but when I call I'm told no. So where is Kiril?

There's one place I haven't checked. I give my buddy-with-benefits Ruslan Omelechko at the medical examiner's a ring, provide Kiril's name and approximate date of disappearance. Ruslan checks and says Kiril hasn't come his way.

"I get off at eight," he tells me.

"I'll buy you an ice cream," I say. "After that, your treat."

There's a short pause. "The part with the ice cream isn't really necessary," he tells me.

I laugh, but when I hang up I'm thinking, Kiril Akhmentov the drug addict didn't move, he *disappeared.*

PART III - Boyko

End of October, it's a balmy day owed for a rainy autumn, and I'm driving my Volga to Linden Tree Farm in the Vyshhorods'kyi district. My father took me skeet shooting when I was a resentful, fumbling teen; I was no good whatsoever, and anyone who has a short-tempered parent will understand why.

"Rustic" Linden Tree Farm is west of Kiev, part of a rural expanse where hedgerows line rain-soaked fields and it's advisable not to leave the highway without four-wheel drive. I steer the Volga toward a huddle of ramshackle sheds; two dogs on chains welcome me with tepid tail wagging. A lopsided, grey timbered house peeps through grape vines, sunk nearly to the window sashes as it surrenders centimeter by centimeter to Ukrainian loam, and behind it stands a neat two story house of fresh yellow logs, a plastic sink is bracketed to the side of an outhouse wall, a satellite dish is wedged in a tree, and there's a shiny new outdoor grill. No sign of anyone. Further on a rutted crescent provides parking for a pair of vehicles and I nose the Volga alongside. I hear bursts of small arms fire nearby. I have a 12 gauge I've borrowed from my brother-in-law Ilya, which I retrieve from the back seat, then I tramp along the border of a boggy lane.

Two men and a woman, backs turned to me, are firing on targets within an open sided shed. I trudge onward. Up ahead there's a scruffy woodland of pines and birches, not a linden tree anywhere, although I wouldn't know a linden if one fell on me. I find another parking lot, this one graveled, with several more vehicles including a school van. What the hell? Does school van mean what I think it does?

I'm suddenly nervous at the prospect of competing against secondary school students. I didn't have a fun time during my formative academic years, and there's residual psychic damage. Sure enough, kids are spilling out of the blue school van and heading toward two cinderblock skeet houses and I follow. A handful of adults whom I assume are parents are chatting to one side.

A young man spots me, his rigid bearing suggests a hitch in the military. "Kondrashov?"

"Yeah."

"I'm Vanya," he announces. "There's been a scheduling error. We're conducting student practice."

A twinkly light blinks on. This is Anatoly Kornelyuk's revenge for my nasty behavior at the gun club.

"You're welcome to practice with the kids," Vanya adds, his eyes flicking over Ilya's heirloom gun.   I remind myself to suck it up, that I'm tracing the connection of weapons to a christening massacre.

"I didn't bring shells," I say lamely.

"We supply ammo. You're an experienced shooter, right?"

"Absolutely," I tell him. *Just not with a shot gun,* I don't say.

"Good. Today's group is competing in a national championship next week, I'm sure they'll benefit by observing a pro."

"Great."   I'm up against smart-ass kids with competitive experience. I'm wondering if I should say I forgot my safety glasses in the car, and turn tail.

Pegs are laid out on a cement arc between the high house and the low house. Beyond lies a wide field, oat stubble pokes through flourishing ragweed. The weather has altered in the few minutes since I arrived, clouds are rolling in and a frisky breeze scatters leaves.

Guess who's first?

"Kondrashov! You're up."

I step to station one and load two shells. I raise the muzzle toward a tarnished-silver sky. "Pull!"

A clay from high house beats my barrel and disappears. "Pull!" Next is incoming, I misjudge the lead and the clay soars unscathed above oat stubble.

"I'm rusty," I say with a big fake smile for no one in particular.

I step back, avoid the kids, wait awkwardly with parents. I feel better when the kid after me misses his shots too. Between bursts of gunfire a cricket chorus swells, breaks off, swells again.

All too soon it's my turn again. I return to the station one peg and get schooled.   "Kondrashov-second position!"

The students regard me with bemusement, they have my measure now. Two girls and six boys, the girls in full makeup, one in head-to-toe denim with lime-colored sunglasses, the other in short-

shorts, knee socks and a cherry polyvinyl jacket. The boys are carefully turned out in rock band tee's, windbreakers, jeans.

This time I blast both targets into quantum particles. And the next. The kids relax toward me. Even Corporal Vanya loosens up. The practice drags on for another hour, in the end I don't do badly, although I'm no closer to discovering if the Mouflon Gun Club supplied rifles to the St. Ignatius assassins.

Afterwards I walk back along the lane. The two girls catch up as I pass the bus, offer me a hand-rolled smoke, which I decline. One of them wants to know what it's like to be in law enforcement.

I'm startled and show it, she tells me Vanya the instructor warned they were in for stiff competition from a Kiev cop. She's curious to hear if I'd recommend police work as a career. She sounds serious but who knows: a neck strap holds a heart-shaped stone and makes me think her mind's on other things. But I say yes, things are better now, they've changed their ways.

"Not what I hear," says the other.

I shrug. Before the recent overhaul, Kiev cops had a habit of accepting remuneration in return for linking their fingers behind their backs. "They're working on it."

In the distance a white farm house sits beside a pond.

"That's Boyko's mom's house," says the career-minded girl, following my gaze.

"Who's Boyko?" I ask.

"The owner. His mama has only one arm. She lives alone and does for herself, even milks the cows."

I'm having difficulty visualizing this.

A jeep comes off the main road. I ask if that would be Mr. Boyko?

Silence, as they watch the jeep's progress with appraising stares.

I decide to say hello to Mrs. Boyko. I tell the girls bye and cut across the fields as the breeze builds, and clouds of an unsettling metallic hue roil in the western sky. I'm wondering how Vanya knew I was a cop, then I remember I went to the gun club in uniform, which means Anatoly Kornelyuk gave someone a heads up.

But why?

****

Four cows wade into a pond. That's not the opening line of a joke, the beasts nearly trampled me. (Actually they passed nearby, but cows make me nervous and I don't shrink from slandering them). Once in the water they lift their tails and pee, so I yell, *that's your drinking water, geniuses!*

I follow the curve of the pond toward the farm house, up a slope through an orchard littered with spotty apples, past a lone goat chained to a stake, past a tractor that was new when Ivan the Terrible was still in jammies. A tall man is applying caulking around a window pane beside the back door. Firewood is stacked waist-high along the wall.

"Good afternoon," I say.

"Good afternoon, miss."

I'm suddenly aware that I'm still lugging Ilya's shotgun. "Skeet range," I explain.

He wipes away excess caulking with a rag. The movement is deft, precise. "How can I help you?"

I think of the cows that barged past. "The kids at practice told me I could buy fresh butter," I lie.

He pretends he believes this. "You a local girl?"

"I'm a local cop," I say. "Katya Kondrashov." I'm pretty sure he already knows. People say intelligence shows in the eyes, but I pay heed to the voice, and Boyko's has nuance and subtleties. Something else, he's the owner of a sizeable operation, but he's wearing threadbare jeans, and the collar rim of his plaid shirt is frayed to white.

"Bogdan Boyko," he says. "Why don't I ask my mother if she's churned today?"

He sets the caulking gun atop the firewood, then repositions it, and again a third time, as if he's giving himself time to think.

"Winterizing?" I ask.

"Repairs. My son and I make short work of it."

He pushes the back door inward, removes his boots. "Come in."

"I'll be a bother," I say. There's a twitchy component to Mr. Boyko's energy, plus he's got me by twenty-five kilos. I'm way outmatched if we end up arm wrestling.

"My mother doesn't get many visitors," he insists.

Since it's now a matter of courtesy, I lean the shotgun against the wall, remove my hiking shoes, step into the farmhouse. The interior has the mismatched look of resourceful making-do, everything's crammed in a single room, kitchen, dining table, a fuzzy orange couch, a dusty flat screen, a corner of icons with votive candles. There's a curtain that probably leads to a bedroom. A scrawny kid reclines on the orange couch, knotty biceps on display, knee tattoos exposed by ripped jeans. His straight black hair has a deep part and pompadour, and he's wearing pristine white no-show socks, which he presses against the thighs of a slack-faced female companion. Both are tapping away at their phone screens.

Bogdan introduces me. "My son Philip. His friend Yulia."

I don't bother extending a hand, neither of these two has any interest.

"Where's your Baba Lyuda?" Boyko demands of his son.

"Digging spuds."

Boyko reddens. "You're here to lend a hand."

"Relax, Pop. She asked me to make a grocery run. I need the keys to the jeep."

The kid shifts a yellow object from his belly and sets it aside. It's a moment before I identify it. It's a cattle prod charger. He stands, ducks through the curtain into the back room and I hear drawers being slammed.

"Stay out of your grandma's money!" A flush creeps up Boyko's neck. He pulls a wad from his jeans, peels off bills and when Philip returns he hands them to his son.

Philip pockets the money without comment, then turns back to his girlfriend. He studies her silently, then snaps his fingers. "There's been a development," he says.

The girl doesn't react, and Philip bends over her and begins chanting, no, *shouting* a popular Russian rap song. "гуляем; летаем!" "Gool-YA- em! Leh-TA-yem!" *We walk, we fly*. The languid girl twitches a cheek muscle, then rises and follows him out. I hear the jeep start up.

"Have a seat," says Boyko. "I won't be a minute."

I go to the back door and watch him stride away. Minutes later Boyko returns, carrying a stainless steel bucket, and ushers in a sturdy woman in her seventies, white scarf, black boots, angelic blue eyes, ruddy skin. She's clearly an outdoor girl. Bogdan makes introductions. Mom nods and moves away to wash her hand under a spigot. She's not ambidextrous but neither am I. Asked by Boyko if she's churned butter, she says she's still skimming cream from the milking.

Boyko dumps the contents of the bucket into a sink, and from the thumping I assume they're potatoes.

"I'll be going," I say. "It was a pleasure," I tell Mrs. Boyko.

She nods again. She's saying something, but I don't catch it. Then I do. She's singing to herself in a low voice. It's kind of catchy.

She's singing her grandson's Russian rap song. гуляем; летаем…we walk, we fly…

"My musical mom," says Boyko, unfazed. "You should stay, she'll put a kettle on." I can't tell if he's being ironic, anyway I'm already tugging on my shoes. He follows me out, hefts Ilya's old gun and examines it. "This one could tell stories…"

"It's my brother-in-law's."

He hands it over. "We give a discount to law enforcement officers," he tells me. "Stop by the store in Kiev."

I'm letting an opening slip away, it's now or never, and there's no subtle approach. I take a deep breath. "Have you inventoried at the club recently?"

"You mean guns?"

"I'm wondering if you're missing three rifles."

"No. I've got a pretty good tracking system. Why?"

"A recent incident."

He thinks about this. "You mean the murders in the cathedral."

"Correct."

"Out here in the boonies everyone owns a rifle."

I stand my ground. "The killers would avoid using weapons that could be traced to them."

"You're an investigator? Is that why you're here?"

I think of little Ina's bloody christening. "I'm a road cop, but I've developed a personal interest."

"You're acting on your own?"

"Strictly speaking."

"Strictly speaking, you may be prejudicing a legitimate investigation."

He's right. He's so intense that for a second I worry that I actually *am* interfering with Detective Volodney.

Let's see…. okay, I'm over it.

"Thanks for your time, Mr. Boyko." I'm feeling mildly spooked. Maybe it was the cattle prod charger, maybe it was the one-armed babushka singing rap, but I'm fairly certain it's all on Mr. Boyko.

"I'll let you know about the butter," he calls after me. Again, I can't tell if he's being sarcastic; I'm relieved he doesn't have my phone number, then I remember I gave it at the Mouflon Gun Club when I signed up for skeet.

I jog down through the apple orchard and cut across fields. I don't look back. Five minutes later I reach the car under a black sky. The first tiny pellets of hail are pinging off the hood of the Volga.

Just up the lane, the gunfire from the small arms range has ceased. The two cars from earlier have departed, but now a dark blue Ford Focus is parked beside me.

Ten minutes later I glance in the rearview, and see the blue Ford. I lose it in Kiev's jam-packed downtown traffic.

****

Later that evening I have an inspiration and I call Reverend Mefody Tuchina at St. Basil's Renaissance Rehabilitation. I ask him if he's heard of Kiril Akhmentov, a violent drug offender with a young son. He hasn't.

I say thanks and have a nice day. Evening. Then I call back.

"What about Anatoly Kornelyuk?"

"Tolya is one of our part-time counselors," he says. "He came to us from the Lvov program."

I thank him again and spend a few minutes stroking my cat Masha, who's been mauled by my niece and nephews all day, but submits anyway. Is Kiril the druggie living in Lvov and receiving treatment? Only one way to find out. I call Renaissance Rehab in Lvov, and ask to speak to Kiril Akhmentov; I'm his lawyer and if he misses his court date it's automatic jail time.

The person on the other end tells me I'm barking up the wrong tree.

"Can you at least tell me if he's there?"

A short pause. "I can't comment on the status of current participants in the program," he says carefully.

"That's all I needed to know," I say.

****

Dimitri Nikolaychuk phones the following morning, asking again if he can bring a camera to video the baby.

"You'd be doing me a giant favor," he assures me. "I'll respect any terms you set."

 "Can't help," I say.

"Just me and a tiny camera, you won't even notice."

When I hang up I'm humming Egor Creed's "Bride" again.

PART IV - Baby Ina's Journey of Hope

Tru-Vision and other news outlets are wrangling over contending theories behind the St. Ignatius massacre: it was carried out against grandpa Litvak, for his role with the Berkut riot police, or it was orchestrated by the Odessa Mafia, seeking to squash a freelancer for selling contraband cigarettes from Uzbekistan. The only thing that all sides agree on is that Ukraine has lost control over the movement of arms, and that gun violence is rising precipitously.

Reporters are also pestering Commander Shulikov over the fate of the newly christened baby, but he's not telling, and so far no one has snitched. Sooner or later someone will, and they'll overrun my sister's house.

****

 On my next shift I pull over the mayor's wife for cell phone use while operating a vehicle. She's a courteous woman and her husband was also a hero of the Maidan uprising. I feel bad about writing a ticket, but I do so anyway, otherwise it's a slippery slope.

A few minutes later I answer my own phone while barreling down Naberezhne Highway. It's Bogdan Boyko. Boyko's brought me freshly churned butter from his mother's house. He's in town. He's at Independence Square. I tell him I'm on duty.

"Swing by. I'll hand it through your window like take-away."

Of course he doesn't hand it through the window. He's standing twenty meters from the curb, and he waits for me to walk over. He gestures toward the victory pillar. "That means something. 'Soul and body I will lay down for my freedom.'"

We're surrounded by skateboarders and cyclists who have both freedom and free time, and I'd love to know how they manage it.

"Did you take part in Maidan?" he asks. It's a trick question, because in a way everyone was a part of the uprising against our former Russian-backed government. The real question is which side you were on.

"I don't like crowds," I hedge. I don't tell him my mother came every day for weeks with garden produce and bags of macaroni.

"I learned something. We can do anything if we have the will, and if we act together." This doesn't sound anecdotal, it sounds weighty, and Boyko scrutinizes me for reaction. "I'm more the loner type," I say lamely.

He hands over the butter, it's a smooth round of pale yellow, nearly a kilo, packed in a clear plastic bag with ice. I'm puzzled. His mom churned a kilo of butter overnight? She has an ice machine?

"What's the next step, Katya? Everyone knows in their hearts what we have to do now, but we've backed off. In time we'll forget what we learned here."

For some reason I think of Dubke Park.

"Are we going to let it happen, Katya? All that effort for nothing?" There's a disquieting fervor in his voice, maybe even zealotry. I'm not a fan of zealotry. The French chopped all those necks, and ended up with Napoleon.

I'm edging away. "I'd better get this in the fridge."

"A group of people is meeting at the farm this weekend. I'd like you to come."

"A gun club meeting?"

"It's not about guns. We call ourselves the Mouflons, and we discuss what's happening to our country. There are activities, too. On Sunday we're delivering firewood to elderly residents in my area. We can always use an extra pair of hands."

Now the weird part. He reaches out his hand, and lays it on my shoulder, as if he's about to pull me toward him. I quickly shrug it off.

I say I have to get back to the job. I sense he's not done proselytizing, but I walk away, not even thanking him for the butter. Once in the car I lay down rubber. Boyko's trying to recruit me, I'm not sure for what.

A mouflon, by the way, is a big horned sheep. I think Boyko wants me to be a Mouflon. A ewe, since I'm female.

Maaa...aaa...aaa...

****

Now for the hard part.

At the end of my day I'm summoned to Commander Shulikov's office and told that I'm to bring Irina Litvak to HQ the following morning, where I'll turn her over to a rep from Family Services. Failure to do so will result in immediate suspension. I don't bother Shulikov with protest, he's clearly not in the mood. I drive home with a sick feeling, my brain working manically.

Before I reach home I decide against warning Anna that Ina's time is up; it's better my sister doesn't suspect.

I slip upstairs and glare at a bust of Josef Stalin, a chunk of memorabilia from a previous, more successful investigation. I've failed Ina on every level; I haven't found her a home, and I may never learn who murdered her family. Beaver-toothed Anatoly Kornelyuk turned out to be a part-time drug counselor, who was able to persuade Kiril Akhmentov, a violent addict, to give rehab a shot. And the Mouflon Gun Club proprietor, Bogdan Boyko, is a trifle creepy, but he's also distributing firewood to his elderly neighbors in the countryside. Why do I suspect the worst of people, and feel disappointment when I'm wrong?

Joe Stalin grins at me from the floor, where he does duty as a door jam.

****

I wade through chicory and nettles -the only flowers that flourish in Anna's yard- and place Ina in her car seat, and beside her a bag of diapers, formula, clothing.

I close the door, praying it doesn't set the baby off, but hoping most of all it doesn't rouse my sister. I push back the creaky, squeaky metal gate. Ilya's delivery truck blocks my exit, and I return to snatch the keys from the foyer table, and reverse his vehicle into the street.

A drowsy, barefoot Ilya waits on his doorstep. "Are you stealing my truck, Katya?"

"Go back to bed," I tell him. I toss him his keys.

I fire up the Volga and ease down the drive until I hear a squawk of indignation, and Anna erupts from her house in her bathrobe. I stop as she collides with my door.

"What are you doing, you lunatic? Where are you taking my Ina?"

"She's not yours," I tell her harshly.

"Katya…."

"I'll lose my job," I say.

She tries to grab the steering wheel, but I straight-arm her, she stumbles back, and I gun the car into the street.

Ten minutes later I park my car behind HQ, where I climb in the back and sit with Ina. She's talkative this morning, and we have a good conversation, but I think we're both keeping it light to avoid contemplating a parting of ways.

The Ford Focus that followed me from Linden Farm is parked across the street, after tailing me from my house this morning. I wait another quarter hour, then I carry Ina inside HQ, past personnel lockers and showers, past the open door of Sergeant Dasha's morning briefing, past the closed door of Commander Shulikov's office, and out the main entrance to a VipLux taxi.

****

Yesterday after talking with Commander Shulikov I went online and bought a ticket to Kharkov. The train departs in an hour, and I'll be in Kharkov around two thirty this afternoon.

I have a copy of the christening certificate, obtained by Anna some days ago via an acquaintance at St. Ignatius. I also have four acorns from the erstwhile oaks of Dubke park. The acorns are quite possibly an over-the-top gesture, and will likely return to Kiev in my pocket.

Ina's aunt and uncle are ethnic Russians; the uncle went a little crazy when Donetsk declared independence from the rest of us, and he and his drinking buddies planted a Russian flag on top of a Kharkov post office. The uncle, a coal miner, was tried for subversive activity and has been in jail until three months ago.

Beyond that I don't have anything, meaning I don't know whether he and his wife have children, whether they can take on another mouth to feed, or if Ina will be loved and properly looked after. It's a gamble, but it's the option we've been given, Ina and I. If Ina has blood relatives, that's where she belongs, and even my neurotic sister Anna should grasp that.

We sit on our bench and wait to embark into the unknown. I ought to be feeling butterflies, but I'm calm, the way suicidal people are toward the end.

****

Ina has the window view, strapped in her car seat, and a woman admires her from the facing seat. The baby's name? Irina, I tell her. She looks exactly like her mommy, I'm assured.

Right now Ina's fussing and not at her cutest, since she's missing Anna and the kids. As soon as the train gets underway I take her to the buffet car and ask if they'll heat formula.

When I return the woman in the window seat looks up from her copy of "Networks and Telecommunications" and asks if I know I'm being filmed. I swivel in time to catch Tru-Vision's Dimitri Nikolaychuk leaning over a seat in the opposite aisle, with a pocket size camera aimed my way. Once discovered, he rises and stands over me. "Miss Kondrashov, how are things?" He points to the camera with his free hand. "Discrete and unobtrusive, didn't I promise?" I'm in shock and it must be evident. The telecom lady seems tensed to act on behalf. Dimitri settles precariously on the arm of the seat across from me.

I find my voice. "The blue Ford was yours?" I ask.

"My assistant producer's. I assume you're delivering Irina Litvak to the Russian-separatist relatives in Kharkov." He maneuvers until he's fully seated. His knees graze mine. "There must be a more suitable home for her."

The woman across from Ina is now regarding us with consternation – I'm a baby trafficker, or worse. Perhaps it's her expression, or the presence of the camera, but I begin ticking off the options impatiently: there's a twenty-three-year old unmarried brother of the mom, who luckily for him, was undergoing gall stone surgery at the time of the christening. He was the sole attendee at the funerals of his parents and two sisters. Dimitri already knows this. Tru-Vision was there.

There's the elderly aunt who suffered the loss of her leg. She remains in the hospital in serious condition. No more relatives of the mother. That's it. Finito.

Now for the Litvaks. Their funeral was attended by a few of Mr. Litvak's former colleagues, and by friends of Mrs. Litvak, and by high school friends of Sergei Litvak, the father. No blood relatives among them. I know this because it I watched Dimitri report it on Tru-Vision News at 6:00.

"That leaves the Litvaks in Kharkov."

"What's the word from Family Services?"

I don't answer.

"Miss Kondrashov...." He appears sympathetic, and he's also got that athletic Dynamos body, and I'm finding it hard to hate him. He says, "You're not only going to lose your job, you're probably going to jail."

Okay, now I hate him. "It's not about me."

"I get it. It's about the baby." The camera lingers on my face, and then he shuts it off. I glance up in time to see Dimitri mentally calculating TV ratings numbers, like money signs in a cartoon character's eyes. "I need another five minutes of video inside the Litvak home in Kharkov," he says.

"Good luck with that."

"You're going to help me, Katya."

"Nope."

"In return for getting me in to film the Litvaks, as they welcome baby Irina into their home, I'm going to do you a favor."

"I don't need anything from you."

"I'm going to spill the beans on Bogdan Boyko."

Once again I'm blindsided, even though I now know Dimitri had me tailed from Linden Tree Farm. I must have taken a stupid pill this morning. I'm not ready for Boyko to be anything other than a spooky, self-appointed savior of Ukraine.

I bluff. "Don't bother. I've got him figured."

"Did you know he was in the Berkut?"

My shock is hidden by a wail from Ina, who's being inadvertently force fed because I'm distracted.

My companion the telecom lady looks shocked and unhappy, she obviously finds the whole exchange with Dimitri distasteful. She shifts as if planning to switch seats, but instead pulls a Roshen chocolate bar from her coat pocket, and settles resolutely back down.

****

A fifties era apartment building stands in a row of similar monolithic giants. Rust from balcony railings runs like a drunken girl's eye-liner; in the lobby an electric sconce flickers and buzzes, a hastily applied paint roller blots graffiti. Ina squalls loudly, and Dimitri's camera zooms in on her displeasure.

There's no answer on the nineteenth floor.

"They're passed out under the kitchen table," says Dimitri.

"They're at work," I retort.

"What now?"

I don't have an answer; I didn't think ahead.

"Lunch," Dimitri decides. "You like sushi, right?"

I'm not hungry, I'm mentally exhausted, I ask the cab driver for a hotel, and he drops me off at the Park, a modest hotel with an alpine façade, while Dimitri Nikolaychuk goes in search of a meal.

 I need to sleep. At the very least I need to draw the curtains, lay in darkness, and think things out, because I've blundered, badly.

I'm certain the Litvaks are going to be horrible. I try to strategize how I'll extricate myself and Ina from a massive gaffe. It's not too late to return to the train station, but I feel paralyzed.

I check on the baby, then sprawl on the bed and sink into blackness. I startle awake after dark. It's Dimitri, he's brought borsht in a Styrofoam cup, and blini with black caviar. I eat while we wait for a cab.

****

Back at the apartment tower, a gentleman with a moustache and hooked nose answers my knock on the Litvak's door.

"Mr. Litvak?"

"No, I'm Ivan." His eyes move to the baby.

"I've brought Irina Litvak," I tell him.

"I'll fetch Mikhail. Why don't you step inside?" He motions to a German shepherd mix that's come to the door. "He's a sweetie."

I enter, Dimitri follows with the car seat and diaper bag, we slip off our shoes. Multiple voices compete in a nearby room.

A woman in a green party dress, brown hair, and glasses with thick black rims enters the hallway. Her eyes go to Ina, before flicking back to me with dawning realization.

"I'm Katya Kondrashov," I tell her.

"Is this my niece?" she asks.

"This is Irina Litvak."

"Praise God."

I believe she wants to take Ina, but I don't offer. Instead I introduce Dimitri Nikolaychuk; she doesn't recognize him as a TV reporter, and asks him if he wants to set down the car seat. As soon as Dimitri has a free hand his camera reappears.

"Won't you please come this way?"

A second gentleman now appears in the hallway, late fifties, black hair cropped short, a striped polo shirt. "My husband," says Mrs. Litvak. "They've brought Sergei's daughter," she tells him.

"I'd like to film, with your permission," Dimitri tells Mrs. Litvak. He makes it sound as if he's a close friend, helping me preserve a special moment.

"Mr. Nikolaychuk is a reporter for Tru-Vision," I tell her. "He plans to broadcast a segment about Ina's arrival here in Kharkov."

I clutch Ina protectively, and it's possible that the Litvaks believe Dimitri's obnoxious filming is a condition of my releasing the baby to them.

Mr. Litvak shrugs. "Come in. Let the world see us as we are."

I take three or four steps down a dark hallway, then a right turn into a cramped room where a table has been pulled up to a divan, and two men sit there beside a large white stuffed bear.

"Today's my son-in-law's birthday," explains Mr. Litvak. Chairs along the opposite wall hold three middle-aged women, two more chairs at the far end accommodate another woman and an adolescent boy, on this end a young couple presides, whom I assume are the daughter and son-in-law. The young man is holding a plump infant, a few weeks older than Ina.

The meal is barely underway. Plates of sliced apples, cukes and tomatoes, bread, a mayo packet with spigot, chicken, fish, and bottles of champagne and wine are arranged along the table. The young couple rises awkwardly. I sense in everyone a state of tense expectancy, as if the baby I'm carrying might turn out to be a joke, or a bomb.

"Good evening," I say.

"This is Sergei's daughter," blurts Mrs. Litvak.

Astonished gasps and whispers from the ladies along the wall, while Ina gets her first look at the fat baby in the son-in law's arms, and wails disconsolately.

"Please sit and join us," Mrs. Litvak insists.

Mr. Litvak brings chairs, and himself takes a seat on the divan next to the stuffed bear. The daughter brings champagne glasses for Dimitri and I, and Mrs. Litvak pours bubbly.

At this point I relinquish Ina, and she begins a journey along the wall of seated ladies, who all inspect her in turn. A few minutes later she finds her way back to me.

"We were about to drink a toast," announces Mr. Litvak, "but first I have a special gift for my son-in-law on his birthday."

Mr. Litvak rises ceremoniously and hands his son-in-law a military knife, it's WWII issue, maybe earlier. The young man accepts a coin from his wife and offers it to Mr. Litvak. Next, the eldest of the three ladies along the wall passes the young man a card with cash, well wishes follow, and a toast, in which the clinking of glasses continues until everyone has clinked, including Dimitri and me.

Plates are passed, I nibble a chicken leg, and fill Mrs. Litvak in, as best I can, on Ina's personality traits, her nap times, and her favorite toy, which is a plastic kinder-surprise egg she's fond of mouthing. Mrs. Litvak listens attentively, and Mr. Litvak urges Dimitri to try the herring-in-a-blanket.

Eventually I'm reminded that we're intruding on the lives of strangers, and Dimitri decides he's gotten the shots he needs. He stashes the camera, pokes me with an elbow, and announces that we have a train to catch.

Mr. Litvak rises again, and thanks me in an emotional voice for delivering his niece, and Mrs. Litvak echoes the sentiment, which makes it official: they want and accept Ina, she has a place in their home, and there's no going back.

I'm still gripping Ina; I can't seem to let go. She'll wake in the night to unfamiliar sounds and smells, in the home of strangers, and she's already been forced to experience that once before.

To say I'm torn about leaving her doesn't cover it. I feel a nauseating, vertiginous sense of guilt for abandoning a tiny girl who depends on my protection, who was handed to me in the same hour that her parents died. The person who passes Ina into the arms of Mrs. Litvak is not the real Katya Kondrashov, but a robotic version of Katya whom I don't recognize, don't countenance, and may never forgive.

****

Whenever I'm sleep-deprived I guzzle coffee. The sleeper train to Kiev sways and rumbles through the night, but I've chosen not to rent a berth, instead I down java and wallow in guilt.

"I've made a terrible mistake."

"She'll be fine."

"She won't."

"They're a decent, reliable bunch, and the old ladies will smother her in attention."

"I forgot to leave the acorns," I moan.

"Who?"

"The good-luck acorns from Dubke Park."

"You're not making sense." Dimitri nudges me with his knee. "The Litvaks will make a little Russian out of her, but she'll be a happy little Russian, and that's what I'll tell the Tru-Vision viewers."

I can't believe that Dimitri Nikolaychuk is trying to make me feel better.

"I heard you broke the Galina Klepikov case," he adds.

It's true. It gives me no pleasure to remember, since we all miss Galina's syrupy, old school advice on our morning radio broadcasts.

"What put you on to Bogdan Boyko?" Dimitri inquires.

"Boyko is a peripheral oddity. It's about Kutsenko, the priest." I rouse myself from self-pity long enough to explain my theory. I'm not leaking confidential information, because Detective Volodney has already solved the case to his satisfaction, which is that the Odessa mafia was responsible.

Dimitri quickly shoots down my idea that the priest was the target. "They didn't kill seven people over park benches," he assures me.

He tells me about Bogdan Boyko, former member of the Berkut riot police, and I'm too buzzed on caffeine to find any of it surprising. Imprisoned after Maidan, Boyko faced charges of beating and torturing protestors, but claimed he was merely in charge of a weapons storage depot. He passed a lie detector test, and was set free pending further investigation.

The investigation by the Prosecutor General continues to gather evidence, two years later.

Boyko wasted no time in remaking himself, says Dimitri with a wry smile. The former Berkut underwent a fanatic conversion, taking over the family gun store, becoming a community and charitable organizer, and religiously attending Alcoholics Anonymous meetings.

The latter, because previously he'd been infamous for drunken shenanigans, and was twice demoted in rank. Dimitri claims Tru-Vision has video of Boyko's car wedged under an asphalt spreader, like a cockroach caught by a cupboard door, after smashing through barriers on the Darnyts'kyi Bridge. A year later Boyko's wife abruptly disappeared, and she remains listed as a missing person.

It all seems like stale news, and none of it brings me closer to learning what happened at St. Ignatius. Around midnight, after my eighth cup of coffee, I rest my head against the window and sleep.

****

I'm grounded for two weeks; further disciplinary action awaits review. Commander Shulikov relays his decision dispassionately, but it's clear he's seen Tru-Vision's *Baby Ina's Journey of Hope*, and he concludes with a stern assessment.   I'm a limelight ranger, and the commander harbors doubts about my future in the department. I leave his office with my tail between my legs.

At home my sister Anna is breezily courteous, the same treatment she gives trolley conductors and Cash and Carry clerks. I imagine that in secret she's sharpening a kitchen knife to slice through bone.

My relationship with my mother is sundered. I've delivered an innocent into the slavering jaws of the enemy. Nothing more to say. Ever.

I should explain that in my mother's parlance "nothing more, ever," means she won't call me for a couple of weeks.

PART V – Linden Tree Farm

My day with the Mouflons begins at 6:00 AM with a cup of tea in the yellow log house, where Vanya the skeet instructor lays out the day's schedule. The Mouflons will spend the morning chopping and delivering firewood throughout the area, followed by lunch, followed by a political discussion led by Bogdan Boyko. There are thirty people present, give or take, the house's small main room is SRO and the attendees wind around a short hallway and onto a covered porch where they listen through a window.

It's drizzling. A sprawling mountain of branches and stumps on the opposite side of the lane has been collected, donated, or trucked in, and must all be reduced to furnace size. Boyko has brought a chainsaw, and Mouflon members have furnished three more. I'm part of a detail which stacks the finished product into cords, before another team loads the two trucks that will deliver.

I was originally invited to join the ladies fixing lunch, but I said for everyone's health and enjoyment it wasn't a good idea. I wasn't joking. Anyway, I've borrowed Anna's gardening gloves, which don't have a smudge of dirt on them, and I'm breaking them in. I'm sure she'll appreciate it.

Scrawny little Philip Boyko, Bogdan's son, has taken the plum assignment for himself. He's driving the tractor, which has a cozy little cabin to keep the rain off. This particular tractor is so old-timey it has iron wheels, with traction cleats along its rims, and it speeds over slick ground without skidding, as Philip is keen to demonstrate. Anatoly Kornelyuk, Tolya, trots behind. My beaver-toothed buddy's in charge of chaining logs behind the tractor, which Philip drags over to the sawing and chopping area. I'm tuned into this because it feels as though these two have a very tense, weird little dynamic going on.

Soon I stop paying attention, because the firewood is unexpectedly heavy, and I've dropped a chunk on my foot.

****

Mid-morning passes just before shouting breaks out across the lane. Bogdan sets down his chainsaw, and strides toward the stacks of trunks and branches. From the tractor cabin Philip is cursing Tolya.

And yes, I'm right behind Bogdan.

"He's totally useless," Philip complains to his father. "We're falling behind because Fat Boy can't keep up." Tolya crouches by the woodpile, panting, teeth bared, resembling a bedraggled groundhog cornered by dogs.

Bogdan listens in silence. He's keeping his cool, and maybe it's because there's a crowd of Mouflons looking on, but I have to admire his restraint. Boyko explains that everyone has to be treated with respect and courtesy, and it sounds like he's addressing all of us. He steps up to the cabin and reaches to place a hand on Philip's shoulder, and I'm close enough to see Boyko's thumb turning white where it's pressed against Philip's collarbone.

Work resumes. An hour passes without incident, but I sense this isn't over. I'm not wrong. Even the buzz of chainsaws can't mask the screams of pain that erupt just before lunch time.

I and others scramble toward the noise of the tractor.

Philip leans from the tractor cabin, face compressed and furious, his pretty haircut in disarray. "It was an accident," he screams at his father. "The fat bastard slipped in the mud!"

Philip has backed over Tolya with the iron wheels, a cleat has cut Tolya's left leg mid-calf, a second cleat shears his right leg above the knee.

Tolya's shrieking nonstop, bloody foam spraying from his mouth, arms thrashing in the mud.

"Tell your son to turn off the tractor, and set the brake," I tell Boyko. "Then get him out of the cabin."

Bogdan hauls Philip out, still protesting, as Vanya runs up.

"We need to leverage the tractor up," Vanya says. Boyko is already calling for sturdy tree branches. When we ease Tolya out, blood sprays over the muddy ground, carrying white fragments of bone. Both legs are partially severed, the muscles sheared. The good news is that Tolya's about to pass out from a steep drop in blood pressure, and his agony will end for the moment.

"I need tourniquets," shouts Vanya.

He and Bogdan loop belts around both the victim's legs, and I find sticks for windlasses. Before it's over Tolya has lapsed into unconsciousness.

****

The patient's been cautiously transferred to an ambulance from City Clinic Hospital # 3, and two paramedics are applying hospital-issue tourniquets above the improvised ones.

I climb inside the ambulance before the doors close. "I'm his wife," I tell them. I lean over Tolya, who's muttering faintly, possibly on the verge of regaining consciousness. The ambulance eases into the rutted lane, and as it turns onto the highway the driver hits the sirens.

A paramedic's filling a syringe from an ampule. "What's in the needle?" I demand.

"Hydromorphone."

I shake my head decisively. "Not for my Tolya. He'll swell like a puffer fish."

Tolya eyelids flutter and he moans, "No...no...please god."

"He's going to need sedation, ma'am."

"Please...the pain..." rasps Tolya.

"Darling, you're awake. Talk to me. Tell me about St. Ignatius Cathedral."

"What? No!"

I whisper. "The pain will stop."

"But...I didn't." His eyes open glassily, stricken and pleading. "I could...didn't..." he stutters and splutters. Reddish saliva spills over his lips.

A paramedic lays a cautioning hand on my shoulder. "Ma'am, he needs to remain quiet."

"Let it out," I prod Tolya.

"I couldn't. I fired...fired... baptismal font. Philip says....coward....betray...."

"Betray Philip and Bogdan?"

"Not Bogdan. Vanya...Philip. Me." He whimpers, clenches his jaws. "My legs. My...freaking...legs."

"The rifles?"

"Vanya. I don't know.... They don't trust...."

"On the farm?"

A visceral squeal of agony escapes Tolya's throat. I take this as a yes. "Shoot him up," I tell the paramedic.

"You said he was allergic."

"My mistake," I say.

I phone HQ and advise them that the deer rifles used in the cathedral massacre are cached somewhere on Linden Tree Farm. I provide directions. I suggest they arrest Philip Boyko and a Mouflon captain by the name of Vanya.

I ask as a favor, could someone swing by City Clinic Hospital # 3 and pick me up?

****

Vanya is in cuffs, but Philip Boyko is missing. His father Bogdan Boyko's in a holding cell at HQ, awaiting questioning.

The buildings on Linden Farm have all been painstakingly searched, but no luck. At old Mrs. Boyko's little dwelling nearby, chicken coops and rabbit runs are torn apart, and the pond is dragged by divers. It's getting late and growing dark.

Commander Shulikov is ordering people back to HQ. I'm feeling slightly sick because the situation is looking grim, meaning we lack evidence to corroborate Tolya's story, which was extracted under sketchy circumstances.

The commander knocks on Mrs. Boyko's door to inform her that we're wrapping up and on our way. Mrs. Boyko is watching TV with a tray on her knees and a bowl of soup. Commander Shulikov shakes his head. "Poor woman," he mutters for my benefit. He raises his voice and apologizes at length to Mrs. Boyko.

I hear her humming between spoonfuls. The commander shoots a look my way, raises his eyebrows.

I recall the first day I met Mrs. Boyko. "She gets a song stuck in her head," I explain.

I turn to leave, and that's when I recognize what Mrs. Boyko is humming. *Dee-lee dee-lee, tra-lee vah-lee.*

It's the chorus to a song my nephew Klem was singing a few days ago, about pitching in with the potato harvest.

As soon as we're outside I seize Shulikov's arm. "She's trying to tell us the guns are buried in the potato patch."

"Nonsense, Constable."

"She can't tell us directly; she'd be ratting out her family. The poor old thing has a conscience, and I think you got to her, Commander."

The appeal to his people skills does the trick. "I suppose it can't hurt to check," he concedes.

****

It's past midnight. The commander's SUV headlights are growing dim, but are still bright enough to illuminate relentless sheets of rain. We are both drenched and muddy. The commander's boots squelch with every step; his uniform has the appearance of soggy blue cardboard. I can no longer think or move, I'm shivering too violently.

The commander and I have taken turns with old Mrs. Boyko's pitch fork. We've turned over the entire field. We haven't found any guns.

But we *have* dug all Mrs. Boyko's potatoes for her.

PART VI – First Snow

The weather boffins have twice given false hope for the season's first snowfall. A day in mid-November is promising, but ends up raining, then sleeting. On the twentieth a second storm passes to our west. Everyone mentions how the children are disappointed, but I'm convinced a few adults feel saddened as well, because I'm one of them.

Philip Boyko is on the run. He took off during the raid on Linden Tree Farm and has evaded searchers. Not my problem, by the way. My suspension has been lifted on the condition I stay clear of the St. Ignatius case.

Also by the way, the rifles used in the St. Ignatius massacre were discovered by the detectives who arrested Vanya. He hid them in his closet, under his boxes of toy soldiers.

Tolya's been talkative, especially when his morphine drip is interrupted. He claims the murders at St. Ignatius Cathedral were a test to see whether they could carry the Maidan revolution to the next level. Risking life and limb didn't cut it anymore. Braving tear gas and water cannons was passé.

You need to be willing to kill, says Tolya.

It was shy and retiring Tolya who suggested that the Kutsenkos deserved to have their heads blown off. The company owner, Vitaly Kutsenko, traveled everywhere with bodyguards, but his brother was a priest at St Ignatius, and vulnerable.

Philip Boyko picked the Litvak christening. He assured the other two that Litvak, like Kutsenko, was a perfect target. Exactly why Litvak was a perfect target only Philip knows, and as I've said, he's on the run.

A psychologist at Tru-Vision suggests that the killing of the elder Litvak, a Berkut commander, was a cathartic moment for Philip Boyko. After a lifetime of Bogdan Boyko's neurotic behavior, and the disappearance of his mother, Philip was trying to kill his own father, by proxy.

I'm not sure I agree. Having met Philip Boyko personally, I don't think he'd have any problem doing the real thing.

None of the above concerns me. I have a crisis to handle.

I have to buy a dress.

****

In the past I've worn dresses, I'm not a total savage, but they remain an alien article of clothing. I'm already second-guessing my decision to wear one tonight, but I did find something nice at "Annette Görtz," and it would be a shame to waste.

My sister remains on her lofty perch; still treating me to the bogus courtesy act. Guess what? I'm fine with that, because she's far too mettlesome.

I'm zipping up when I hear stealthy footsteps on the stair. Moments later Anna sidles in. "I've fetched Masha," she says coolly. "You can't expect us to mind your cat every minute."

This is hilarious, since Masha is the main plaything of Anna's children.

"You're right," I say. "I'll keep her here." Anna is staring open-mouthed at my shimmering dress, my strappy shoes. I reach for a bottle I selected from a display at Agente-Parfumer, and dab strategic areas.

"Are you going out?" Anna asks offhandedly. She drops Masha on my bed. "You never go out."

I don't reply. I lift my coat, slip it on, snag my keys, and gingerly negotiate the stairs in high heels. As I descend, my sister's voice rises in pitch. "Who are you meeting? Someone I know?"

I reach the downstairs entrance, open the door.

"Tell me what's going on, Katya!" Anna shrieks.

She's back to normal, but I don't have time to fill her in. In fact, I think I'll wait a few days to forgive her.

As I reach my car I'm humming "Bride," and the November snow is flying on a brisk and biting wind.

CHAPTER FIVE - THE CRANE GRAVEYARD
-A Constable Katya Investigation-

Part I – Oksana

"Katya?"

"Not now, I'm working."

The voice on the phone belongs to a juvenile, whose name I don't know.

"You'll be kicking yourself," she warns. "It's not too late…"

I punch the horn in staccato bursts as a city bus cuts me off.

"I didn't catch that," I say.

"It's not too late to save her."

I lower a window. The soot-smeared lid of a flame-broiler morning stifles the city of Kiev, but it seems we're in luck. A shift in the weather looms. Clouds stream across the Dnieper and displaced swaths of sunlight race southward on Mykhaila Hrushevskono Street.

The girl may require assistance. "Are you in trouble?"

"Not me," she answers. "Someone you know."

My mystery caller is playing games. I thumb the phone icon off.

****

A deeper murk than usual pools near the Cabinet of Ministers, and a street-baked bouquet of benzene gives way to the crisp scent of imminent rain. I swerve onto the sidewalk at the entrance to Mariinsky Park, abandon my patrol car, and jog eastward along a broad footpath. Green acorns crunch underfoot, and the first raindrops patter among the leaves. I've gained weight recently and it's slowing me down, but fortunately I'm not heading to an emergency.

A gyro-scooter has collided with an ice cream pushcart. I locate the vendor, a wheezing old-age pensioner, as he struggles to right the cart.

"They're long gone," he tells me. "Too-little-too-late; that's the Kiev Police."

"I'll give you a hand." Together we tilt the cart onto its wheels. I lift a striped umbrella and slide it into its bracket, while he retrieves scattered equipment.

"If you could describe the person on the scooter…"

He sneers. "Don't waste my time."

I stoop and recover a green and gold cap emblazoned with the team name *Karpaty Lviv*; he snatches it and kicks loose the wheel lock.

"This will only take a minute," I say evenly.

"You won't nab the hooligans; you couldn't find your tits in a teacup," he says, grasping the handlebar. The cart shudders over uneven paving bricks. He calls over his shoulder, "By all means, write a thorough report."

I'm patient with irascible old men, because my father is one, but I'm also a stickler for rules.

"The thing is, your cart's in violation of footpath regulations. I'll need your ID and vending permit."

Ten minutes later he's on his way again, with my personal gift to the careless and the cavalier of Kiev – a traffic ticket.

I join an exodus of park visitors as the rain intensifies, and my mobile rings as I approach my car. I take a deep breath for patience, slide behind the wheel, and fumble with an ear bud.

"Katya?" the girl asks.

"I'm Officer Kondrashov to you."

"I thought we were friends."

"My friends don't play nasty little phone pranks." I nose the car into traffic and stomp on the accelerator.

There's silence on the other end, and I'm on the verge of hanging up when she says, "Something has happened and I wanted to warn you." Her tone is defensive and I believe I may have ruffled her feathers. "That's what a friend would do."

The connection ends. I estimate she's very young; ten years old at most. I check as always for caller ID, but as always, she's switched it off.

****

If Genghis Khan were free to babysit, he'd be standing in my sister's kitchen, asking where the nappies are stacked. Instead, Anna has plumbed the deep end of her option pool, and called me. (I rent the second floor, so essentially she yelled upstairs).

"Fruit for snacks," says Anna, taking finicky care with her press-ons as she tugs at the refrigerator door. "No ice cream, and don't order pizza." Her hair is pinned up, her summer dress strains to contain her bosom, and she's four centimeters taller in the heels I loaned her. (I predict I'll never get them back).

"Tangerines and apples, already sectioned." She indicates a container. Her youngest boy Vanya rushes the open refrigerator; she spins him 180°, and he lurches goofily away.

"I'll manage!" I insist, as Anna's husband Ilya appears behind her in slacks and dress shirt, smelling of aftershave. I throw up my hands. "I can't stand it, you're both too sexy."

My sister preens. "Thanks, Katya. I'll bring back a slice of cheesecake." I'm fairly certain she's telling me I'll be paid in cake, not cash.

Anna and Ilya head for the door, and the children squeal in protest, as if they hadn't been told repeatedly that mommy and daddy were spending an evening out.

****

An hour later I'm making pizza (we've eaten all the ice-cream) when Anna's home phone rings. It's the police. In fact, it's my supervisor, Sergeant Dasha, wanting to speak to my brother-in-law Ilya.

"I tried the Melnyk residence," says my sergeant. "No answer." She means Ilya's parents.

I should ask what's wrong, but I'm afraid to, so I pretend Sgt. Dasha is phoning for social reasons. "It's the Melnyks' wedding anniversary," I say. "They've booked a banquet room at the Premier Palace." As I wait for my supervisor to continue, I brace for bad news.

"A young female's been found dead," says Sgt. Dasha. "According to her ID card her name is Oksana Melnyk."

"It's a mistake," I say. "She's at the party."

Sgt. Dasha waits for me to process before providing details. "I'm sorry, Katya," she finishes. "If there's anything…."

"I'm heading over," I interrupt. I hang up. Anna's teenage sister-in-law, Oksana Melnyk, has been discovered dead at the Crane Graveyard, an industrial junk yard on the south end. My gut churns, my hands are shaking.

In the kitchen Vanya and Klem apply cheese slices to the pizza-in-process. My niece Nadia had first crack, spreading the sauce, and diminutive red handprints pattern the table edge. I pick up my mobile, put it down. I pick it up again, call my sister.

"What's happening?" she asks, overly merry. She hasn't partied in a zillion years, and I'm guessing the drinks are hitting her hard.

"It's Oksana," I tell her. "Ilya's sister."

"She's not here yet," laughs Anna.

"Put Ilya on, okay?"

A pause. "What is it, Katya?"

"Put Ilya on," I repeat. I listen as Anna's breathing changes tempo; comprehension is filtering through the alcohol haze, and finally she says okay, and I hear Ilya's voice.

Forty-five minutes later I'm waiting at a window when the street gate slides back, Ilya's car pulls in, and another vehicle following will be Ilya's parents. I've put the children to bed, and I've crammed a flashlight, gloves, pepper spray and a gun in my shoulder bag. I head out into the yard. Before I make it to my car Ilya's dad emerges from his, and he stumbles a bit as he hurries toward me. "I'm coming with you," he says.

"No way. It's a crime scene."

"Katya, I have to know."

"I'll call you as soon as I can," I promise. He grips my arm and I freeze; I wait a few beats until he releases me. Then I fire up the Volga, back into the street, and lay down rubber.

****

The rain of earlier has eased and fog dims and distorts the street lighting. As I drive I'm thinking of Anna's in-laws, who've been trying Oksana's cellphone non-stop since I called Anna at the Premier Palace, and who insist Oksana's at a friend's, her phone's off, and she missed the anniversary party because her medication leaves her confused.

After speaking with Sergeant Dasha, I believe there's little possibility that a mistake's been made.

The Crane Graveyard lies beyond the Southern Bridge, and east of the Metro Highway, fenced in by prefab concrete slabs. I park on the access road and make my way to a chain link gate where I show a badge. I note that the primary light source is illumination from the adjacent roadway, meaning the place is unused during night hours.

Once past the entrance I follow a graveled corridor; on either side are arrayed stacks of grated walkway, crane sections, loose coils of wire rope, and piles of concrete ballast slabs and counterweights. The corridor ends at an offload area, where a tower crane bends at the waist above a little pick-and-carry, as if issuing instructions.

An officer waits behind a cordon of yellow tape, I show my badge again and slog through puddles toward the portable scene lights on the east side.

The body's covered by a blue tarp, and the immediate area is a bog of roiled mud. Mister Rudskoy and Mister Bumchik stand a few feet off; they're solid detectives, and I provided Spanish translation on a recent case involving guest workers. They turn as I approach.

"Miss Kondrashov."

"I can ID," I say.

"Sure," says Rudskoy. He bends and draws back a corner of the tarp. It's Oksana, she's lying on her left side, the right side of her face appears to have been bludgeoned.

Rudskoy replaces the tarp. "What do you know so far?" I ask.

What Rudskoy knows is that Oksana was struck with a loose wedge of cement, she fell backward and caught the base of her neck against a stack of grated walkway. The piece of cement has been recovered, with blood trace. All footprints in the area belong to the crew that unloaded ballast sections at around 14.50 in the afternoon, and subsequently discovered the body.

Bumchik points to a yellow handbag. "There's cash in the wallet, but no phone," he tells me. "Is she a relative, Miss?"

"Oksana is my brother-in-law's younger sister."

"No signs of sexual assault," says Ivan Rudskoy.

Rudskoy continues. About two-thirty in the afternoon the crane operator arrived to offload a trailer, climbed up to the crane cab, and from that vantage spotted a figure lying amid the rain puddles inside the eastern fence. He alerted the men in the truck, and all three walked over to investigate. That's how Oksana was found.

"She ever mention this place?" asks Mister Bumchik. He motions with his chin toward the lone working crane in the Crane Graveyard. A pair of lights blink at the top to alert small aircraft, and behind the crane, across the highway, electro-transmission towers strobe with warning beacons.

"Not to me." I feel inadequate because they're expecting me to fill in the blanks.

"It's a hangout for kids," Rudskoy supplies. "They squeeze under the main gate, or climb over the barricade, easy as *dvajdee dva*. No guard dog to warn them off."

"It doesn't sound like her," I say. I'm also wondering if Rudskoy means she could have been killed by another kid.

Bumchik chimes in. "No other marks, no bruising. She didn't put up a fight."

"I have to call the parents," I say.

I move away, thumb up the Melnyk's number, stand with the phone in my hand.

Out past the main entrance I see a slice of river, faint boat lights and bridge lights, and in the fog-occluded distance glows the western shore of the Dneiper. Here at the Crane Graveyard there are no high-rise apartments in the vicinity, and it's easy to imagine teens coming here for privacy, to climb around, or get buzzed. But Oksana?

I know a fair amount about the Melnyks, Anna gabbles on about them, but I know less about Oksana in particular. She recently turned seventeen, and she'd been finding her last year of school challenging. Also, she had the odd talent of being able to say words backwards, which she demonstrated for me at a birthday party at Anna's. I met her briefly on several other occasions, a sweet girl whom I suspected was smarter than she pretended, and ...shy? Self-effacing?

Ivan Rudskoy has come up behind me. "We'll need to interview the parents."

"I'll let them know," I say. I press the Melnyks' number.

****

I arrive home weary and bleary, and find my cat Masha behaving in feral fashion; at two in the morning she's voicing guttural yowls from beneath my bed.   She's nearly ten months old, and until recently her estrus cycles have been suppressed by injection. At four AM I get up to brew tea, and try to soothe Masha, as if she were simply upset, and not in the grip of powerful hormones.   She glares and hisses, and ultimately throws herself clawing at the window glass as if she preferred death over human stupidity.

I slurp tea, rummage through the fridge for snacks and find nothing, and then sprawl on the bed and try to recall the exact words of the phone call I received yesterday at Mariinsky Park.

"Something has happened. I wanted to warn you."

My pre-adolescent caller likes to tease. She likes to be ambiguous. The first time we spoke she asked if I knew her grandmother. "I think you ran into her last summer. We both know how that turned out."

Little-girl phone games.

I marshal what I know of Oksana Melnyk, and ask myself again how she might have ended up at the Crane Graveyard, but the little I know is impermeable, smooth as ivory, no way in. I turn on the TV, looking for Oksana's murder in the news feed, but it's too early.

The Melnyks were interviewed last evening, and have given Misters Rudskoy and Bumchik a list of schoolmates and friends. The Department will ask for the public's help during a morning newscast, and we can hope that someone will phone in a tip. My cat Masha approaches stiffly, rubs herself aggressively against my foot, and yowls in anger and yearning. I can relate.

When I head out for work Anna pops into the downstairs hallway, dark circles under her eyes, and I imagine she's been mourning Oksana.

"Why haven't you spayed your damned cat?" she mutters furiously.

****

I take pride in the role that I and the other road cops play in the safety of Kiev's citizens, but today the city is deficient in fizzle and gloss, and I'm thinking that a single officer wouldn't be missed. A Kiev in which Katya Kondrashov dispenses tickets at the Cinema Deluxe, or mumbles in drunken dreams on a park bench, would be indistinguishable from the present one. I'm a low-level, unexceptional cog in the gnash and grind of the municipal gearbox.

Lunch time, and I've parked my patrol car atop the garage overlooking the ferries, when a gleaming new Audi pulls alongside, its door opens and a news reporter from Tru-Vision emerges, approaches my vehicle and slides in on the passenger side.

"My birthday's coming up," Dimitri Nikolaychuk says without preamble, "and I like expensive presents."

I stiffen defensively. "Is this how it's going to be?"

"Clearly you've never had a high-maintenance boyfriend," he tells me. "I'm counting on you to make it a special day."

I nearly choke on my ham and tomato roll-up.

"Is that a 'yes'?" asks Dimitri.

I swallow. "If you're expecting me to sing Happy Birthday…."

He reaches to squeeze my thigh reassuringly. "Lucky you. That's not what I have in mind." He slides out and returns to his car, and pulls away with a horn toot.

Utterly juvenile, I know, but I start feeling special again.

****

End of shift, I drop by Detective Ivan's desk for an update. "Her friends say she changed," he says. "A year ago she slipped off the social radar; no one's sure why."

"Changed how?"

He makes a gesture with his hands. "She didn't talk anymore. Lost her smile and kept to herself. All the rest that you'd expect from a teen in crisis…grades nose-dived, gave up sports, frequent sick days."

This is more serious than what I've gleaned from Anna.

"Any phone tips?"

"A security guard may have noticed a parked car; we'll learn more today." He shoots me a look. "This is not for public consumption, Miss," he adds.

"I'm aware. Don't be a jerk."

"I'm just saying." His tongue darts over his upper lip, is quickly retracted, and he grins. "I heard you made a friend in the media."

"Not true," I lie.

He pokes me in the shoulder, and it hurts. "You keep this stuff bottled up, it starts to fester." He grins some more. "You know I'm a good listener…."

"I haven't a clue what you're talking about." I walk away, really steamed, thinking what a pack of lowlife gossips I work with.

****

I arrive home to find Masha drugged and lethargic in her window basket, her belly shaved and sutured.

"Oh, sweetie!" She opens her eyes stickily, and I choke up. I race downstairs to confront Anna.

"I was going to have her bred, just once, so she'd know," I say, breathless with anger.

Anna is granite. "In that case you should have moved into someone else's house."

This is the real Anna; in case you're wondering. She possesses my mother's lucid sense of right and wrong, coupled with my father's ability to act with swift remorselessness.

I turn on my heel before I get physical, and rush back upstairs. "You owe me nine thousand Hryvnia for spay surgery," shouts Anna.

There's one thing I have that Anna doesn't, which is the ability to hold a grudge for an indefinite time, so I hope she had her heart set on buying something really unique and special with the nine thousand Hryvnia.

Part II - Sasha

The Melnyks have a concern, which they are reluctant to mention to the police. They wonder if Oksana's ex-boyfriend should be investigated.

This is the first I hear of Alexander "Sasha" Yegoshin.

It's Lydia Melnyk, Oksana's mother, who phones. Her voice is hoarse, her speech uneven, and she emphasizes her concern about Oksana's unique vulnerability. She's verging on incoherence. Is this a grief fantasy? I tell her I'll drop by after work, and she thanks me effusively.

It's inexplicable, but I don't remember visiting the Melnyk home, although I think it's where Anna and Ilya held their engagement party, so I must have gone. I rarely block out entire episodes of my life unless they involve boyfriends.

Lydia and Karl Melnyk live ten minutes from Anna's, in a countrified and pricey neighborhood – tall stone fences, fruit weighing the apple boughs, painted daisies bordering a mosaic walkway. Lydia stands in the yard, hands cupping opposite elbows, and she leads me inside where tea and cinnamon cookies wait in the kitchen. She tells me her cat knocked over an electric fan, which struck a pitcher of ice water, and she's just finished mopping up. "What else will go wrong?" she asks ruefully.

I pat her wrist when she takes a chair across from me, and we sit briefly in silence while she gathers herself. Moments later, without urging, she lays out the following story.

In late August, a year ago, her daughter Oksana spent four days at the dacha of a school-friend, and when she returned she was sporting a purple bruise along her jaw and scratches and bruises on both hands. She claimed she'd been helping with gardening, but the explanation was given listlessly and without details. Soon afterwards the Melnyks learned that she'd broken up with her boyfriend of several months, Sasha Yegoshin. At that time, Lydia and Karl wondered if the bruises were related to the break-up, but refrained from asking, because a more onerous change had manifested. Oksana's mood and personality imploded, and eventually her parents arranged counseling with a therapist.

Lydia takes a shaky breath, and searches my face. I don't have an immediate reaction, but I'm curious. I ask about the dacha where Oksana spent the four days.

It was owned by the parents of a schoolmate named Elizaveta, states Lydia. "The sweetest girl, she and Oksana were like sisters."

And Yegoshin, the boyfriend? Lydia rises and excuses herself, and returns with a pale blue phone with a patina of glitter. "We bought her a 6s, her old data was transferred electronically from this one." She hands it over, tells me the password is "Pickles" and I open a photo app and briefly scan pictures until I find a blond boy with his arm slung over Oksana's shoulder. "Him?" I ask. Lydia confirms.

Sasha Yegoshin seems small for a fifteen-year-old, his face is distorted as he mugs for the camera. His friends are laughing and so is Oksana, and I get it. He's comic relief, and if I have this right, he's the opposite of Oksana.

When a shy girl gets attention from the star of her group, she can fall in love, hard.

I place the phone on the table top. "How can I help?"

"My husband and I need to know what changed her. It can't be unrelated. I shouldn't ask you, but you've looked into other...deaths."

"I'm limited in what I can do," I caution. "I can't interfere." (I've interfered egregiously in the past, and received suspension, which I don't mention.) I ask to take the phone with me and she slides it back.

"What do you know about the boy's parents?"

"Only what Oksana told us. The father's an aide to the mayor. The mother manages a grocery store on the east side. Voskresenka, I think."

"I know the police have interviewed you, but can you tell me where she was going on Saturday when she went out?"

"She'd signed up for a work group at the botanical gardens, at the University of Kiev. It was an all-morning affair. Afterwards she hoped to audition for a theater group on campus."

"And she showed up for the work group?"

"Yes. I called her a little after nine. Everything was fine. As the day went on I got caught up with preparations for the anniversary party. We didn't expect to see her until that evening, at the Premier Palace. When she was late I called, but her phone was off. I thought she must be on her way."

Her face twists with guilt, and I know she's thinking *if only...if only...*

In fact, by evening it was too late.

I promise to ask questions about Oksana's traumatic weekend last August, and that's the best I can do. After that we sit in silence, and polish off the plate of cinnamon cookies. I can't think of anything to say that will comfort Lydia; the only comfort for the mother of a murdered child is that the killer will be caught.

****

The burdock below my window has an expansionist agenda, even world dominion may lie within its aspirations, and at shoulder height it threatens to nudge the house sideways. My brother-in-law Ilya has acquired a new weed wacker to vanquish this aggressor, and he's presently hard at it.

I open my window, yell down. "Try using an axe!"

He switches off his stupid gizmo and mops his brow. "What fun would that be?"

I shake my head and prepare to withdraw, but my cat Masha is sticking her head out now.

"Are you going to talk to Anna ever again?" asks Ilya. "She feels guilty about the cat."

This time I pull my head in, and Masha's too, and slam the window.

****

I peruse the photos on Oksana's phone until I find a girl I believe to be Elizaveta. She's one of those girls whose facial contours suggest fragile sweetness: black eyes, black ringlets of hair, a small fox face. Her voice matches up when she answers her phone, whispery with shy courtesy, much like Oksana.

I think: two gentle girls brought together in grade school, who became best friends.

"I'm calling on behalf of Oksana's mother," I explain. I proceed to ask about the weekend at the dacha. More specifically, how Oksana got banged up.

"It's a little blurred," she tells me.

I suppress a sigh. I've already guessed that the dacha story was a cover.

****

Elizaveta confesses that Oksana was never at the dacha, but had gone to the Sorochintsy fair in Poltava with Sasha Yegoshin. The fair hosts offerings by the Poltava Drama Theatre, and Oksana wanted to see plays, as she'd caught the acting bug. From Poltava, Oksana sent texts and pictures, she'd met and chatted with several actors in a play.

The messages from Poltava were the last Elizaveta received. When Oksana returned to school in September she wouldn't talk about any of it, beyond admitting that she'd broken up with Sasha. The yellowish remnant of a bruise ran along her jaw, poorly concealed by makeup.

Elizaveta says she wasn't entirely surprised. Sasha was volatile. He'd been kicked out of his house after fighting with his dad, and was staying with a schoolmate, Misha.

"When was he kicked out?"

"Before they left for Poltava." Does she know where Sasha is now?

"He hasn't been in school, and everyone says he's in Belarus."

"His family moved?"

"Just Sasha."

"He's a child."

"I don't know the details. Misha was showing people a picture of Sasha in front of a fountain in Minsk."

I ask if she knows why Oksana and Sasha were fighting. There's silence on the other end.

"Elizaveta? I need your help."

"I have to go," she says.

"I need Misha's last name."

"It's Grojsman."

"One more thing..." I'm recalling a phrase Lydia Melnyk used to describe Oksana. "Why would Oksana's mom say she was *uniquely vulnerable*?"

"She had panic attacks," Elizaveta responds immediately.

I'm caught slightly off guard, but I feel Elizaveta is waiting for a response. "What was that like?"

"She completely lost her mind." This time she hangs up.

I gently massage my cat Masha along her spine. She's grown visibly plumper since her surgery, which may have something to do with the treats she's constantly offered. "You will never know the joys of motherhood," I warn. Her purr abruptly increases in volume.

I now have suggestions from two sources that Oksana was physically battered by her boyfriend Sasha Yegoshin last year, and at this point I should be calling Detective Ivan with what I've learned. I'm going to do that. However, this boy Misha, with whom Sasha was living after his father threw him out, may be able to shed light. I'm just waiting on that, and then I'll definitely, definitely, call Ivan Rudskoy.

****

On a Saturday I ring Misha Grojsman's phone number and leave a voicemail, and say I'd like to ask about Sasha Yegoshin. An hour later I call again, and an adolescent male voice tells me that Misha's not available, he's at the dentist. When will he be available? I inquire. The connection ends.

 I call the Grojsmans' home phone and say I'm Ilya Melnyk's sister-in-law, I'm putting together a memorial montage for Oksana Melnyk, I'd be deeply appreciative if Misha contributed photos or video. Misha's mom expresses condolences; do I have an address where she can send a card? I give her the Melnyk's address and steer her back to Misha. Her son's at the Natalka Park amusement center, she tells me, and she'll ask him to contact me when he comes in.

I loved Natalka Park when it was wilder; now they've installed walkways and fountains, but it's still the best place to walk among the trees and view the river. I've jogged from Anna's house, and I pause on one of the pathways in the park, to take another look at a group photo from Oksana's phone, with Sasha Yegoshin, Misha Grojsman and two others. Misha is slightly overweight; his expression is bland: a huggable puppy. I cross the street, pay an entrance fee at X-Treme-Attractions, and I'm speculating that soft little Misha won't be exerting himself, which rules out the rock climbing wall, the trampolines, and the roller skating rink.   That leaves the bumper cars. I'm wrong. He's at the ice-cream kiosk with two other boys.

"Is it true you're the fellow with a line to Sasha Yegoshin?"

He regards me incuriously, face placid as a duck pond. "Are you a cop?"

I explain that my sister is married to Oksana's older brother. "I need to know if you or Sasha had spoken with her recently."

He returns to his ice-cream. I don't think he's processing, or delaying, he's simply finding that creamy strawberry taste more interesting than me.

"I haven't talked to Oksana for a while," says Misha, when he surfaces for air. It's not clear whether he knows Oksana's been murdered.

"What about Sasha Yegoshin?"

He starts to walk away.

"Misha? When was the last time you heard from Sasha?"

He turns back. "A few months. He's busy with new friends."

"Do you know where he is now? An address?"

"He's in Minsk."

"And you haven't seen him recently?"

He shakes his head, licks his cone.

"Exactly when was the last time?"

"He was going to the waterpark in Kobleve."

"This summer?"

"Last summer. After that he tuned out."

"Did he give a reason for going to Minsk?"

"A kid he knew moved there."

"Which kid?"

"The kid who played synthesizer in band."

"Could you call Sasha now? Right now?"

"He only answers texts."

"Why's that?"

He shrugs.

"Can you text him now?"

He shrugs again.

"Do you have any texts he sent you?"

Surprisingly he does. I give him my number and with a little prompting, he forwards them laboriously. Next I ask for Sasha's number, which I should have done in the first place.

"The funeral's tomorrow. You should go."

For the first time he reacts to what I'm saying. A flash of incomprehension, perhaps shock, sends a tiny ripple across the duck pond. Something has penetrated his puppy brain. "What funeral?"

"Oksana Melnyk. You were friends, right?"

Relief. "Right. Ok, maybe I'll go." He returns to his treat, crunching the cone.

I wonder, *what was that? That moment of panic?*

I return to Natalka Park, sit cross-legged on the grass, and check out Sasha Yegoshin's texts, which contain three photos, taken in Minsk. I'm not familiar with Minsk and I don't recognize places. Sasha Yegoshin is clowning, as if he hasn't run away from home, isn't on his own in a foreign city without resources, and it's all a prank. I call his phone number. It rings only three times before going to voice mail, so I explain I'm a relative of Oksana and it's urgent he call.

I read the texts, one of which has an attached video from last year, made by Sasha at a seaside resort in Turkey where he's been taken by his parents. The Yegoshin family appears to have the place virtually to themselves, and I assume the Russian tourist ban is in effect or it would be swarming.

The clip begins with Sasha filming himself, alone in his parent's hotel room, where he downs a mug of Finlandia, then swigs from a bottle of Bailey's before heading to the beach. On his way he checks out the petting zoo on the hotel grounds. He's pretending to be childishly excited about seeing the turtles and rabbits, only at the age of fifteen, he's blissfully, perhaps drunkenly uncertain what a duck is and even asks an attendant what it's called. His hair's been dyed, but has grown out. The top layer remains a whitish blond, and he runs his fingers through it constantly with a bemused smile. It's clear that he's pleased with his looks and enjoys filming himself.

The video ends at the pheasant enclosure, whose tenants he finds baffling, eventually deciding they are some sort of chicken.

Technically, he's right.

****

An exceptionally beautiful morning favors the Lukyanovskoye cemetery, drenching it in sunlight, stirring the oak boughs with a north-west breeze. It's crowded. The funeral of a murdered girl is unlike any other; many come to grieve, a few come to soak up the atmosphere. The burial has brought Tru-Vision cameras, too, although I don't see reporter Dimitri Nikolaychuk.

In the main, the attendees are elderly, and I recognize several Melnyks from the christenings of Anna's children. Missing are Oksana's classmates. Elizaveta is here with an older boy, but only a handful of teens mingle with the crowd. Oksana had shut out her school friends, and now they're punishing her.

I scan the assembly in vain for Sasha Yegoshin.

The open casket has caused a good deal of weeping, but Oksana appears content in death, or at least resigned to the circumstance. By now it's been conclusively established that she wasn't the victim of sexual assault, but exclusively the victim of a block of cement.

There's not much more. Oksana went to the site willingly, and was murdered there, swiftly and brutally, and because the weapon was an object at hand, it's unclear if it was planned. There's no trace of her attacker, no cigarette butt bearing DNA, no distinctive size 45 footprint, no suspicious fibers on Oksana's clothing. I know this because my friend Ruslan Omelechko at the medical examiner's told me so.

Why was she at the Crane Graveyard? Did Sasha come back to finish what he started a year earlier?

I realize I've been ignoring the service.

"God will accept her, home, to the kingdom of heaven, to a place where there is no sorrow."

****

Mister Bumchik tells me that on the Saturday that Oksana was murdered, a security guard doing drive-by surveillance noticed a small blue car with white roof parked beside the access road, which he thought might be overflow parking from the cement factory next door. After looking over a catalog of makes and models, the guard's settled on a Mini-Cooper. He didn't take down plate numbers.

Inquiries at the cement factory establish that the Mini-Cooper didn't belong to any of the factory's employees, but could have been a supplier or customer. The factory also posted an ad for employment that week, and several applicants presented themselves.

"How likely that one of them decided to park next door?" I ask the detective.

"Not that far-fetched. Cement mixers hog most of the yard space, and their parking lot isn't paved."

"How many white roofed, dark blue Mini-Coopers in Kiev?"

"At a guess, a couple hundred. Could be from out of town, though."

I believe Mr. Bumchik's telling me it's highly unlikely the Mini-Cooper will be located, which is not the same as impossible, which means he'll follow up.

****

It's after 18.00 when I phone the Yegoshins. I say that I'm trying to gather information about the night Oksana Melnyk was found in the Crane Graveyard, and I'm interviewing her schoolmates.

The woman on the other end hangs up. When I call back no one picks up. This is the third hang-up over Oksana, and it smells funny. If I were a suspicious person, I'd be looking for a rat with its little paws in the air.

Instead I look up the Yegoshins' address. It's in the Obolon district, not far from my sister's house. I don hiking shoes and a windbreaker and walk. It's cool for August and as improbable as it sounds, it's threatening rain again. I stop at a grocer and buy a chocolate bar and savor it, placing little squares on my tongue to melt.

On Obolonksy Prospect a host of massive apartment buildings with trendy "urban villa" architecture have sprung up around Minsk Square, and I press the buzzer at one of these and talk to a man who demands to know if I'm with the police. Instead of answering I repeat that I'm related to the Melnyks.

"We don't know anything," he says curtly, but before he can cut me off I ask if I can speak to Sasha.

"He's not here. You should know if you're with the police, he's been missing for the last year."

"I understand he's in Belarus."

There's silence, and then I'm buzzed in.

The apartment is spacious, grander than I'd expected, and as I remove my running shoes I'm feeling scruffy and underdressed. Mr. Yegoshin is in suit and tie, freshly shaved and cologned, and a woman seated on a divan is giving directions to a taxi company over the phone.

Mr. Yegoshin's agitated, and although I've made clear that I'm making inquiries about Oksana, he wants to hear that there's an active search for his son.

"When did you last see him?"

"He disappeared in August of last year."

"His friend says the two of you had an altercation."

His jaw clenches, he drops his head briefly. Steam vents are whistling, but he's keeping the lid on. "He'd been shoplifting. I smacked his face, he deserved it. I don't know what happened to him -he was always a happy child. We were a happy family."

Suddenly he's inspired and gestures me urgently to follow him. When I'm slow to respond he seizes my arm and pulls me down a hallway, pushes a door open. "Does this look like the room of an abused boy?"

I take it in. It's standard issue for teens these days, electronically equipped and wired, replete with gadgets. Despite a prolonged absence by its occupant, blue and yellow connectivity lights wink dutifully. Computer, sound system, weights, and a trombone all await Sasha's return, as does a reddish cat on the bed. The cat is definitely not abused; in fact, it may be on tranquilizers. It's podgy and languid, it's tongue protrudes a bit from its mouth, and it doesn't stir a hair when I bend to stroke it.

"You haven't heard from him?"

"He went to Minsk," says a grating female voice.

I turn. The mother is there, head cocked as she screws on an earring. "That friend of his, Misha, had a message from Sasha. He'd gotten a place to stay, and a job at a pet store." She straightens and glares at me. "Do you know how many pet stores there are in Minsk? Ask my husband!"

He nods. "Twenty-four. I visited all of them." He sounds betrayed, as if so much searching without result is dismayingly unfair.

Their physical similarity is hard to dismiss. Both are heavy-set, and the wife has a pugnacious stance in keeping with her physique. Mr. Yegoshin, conversely, may have expected life to treat him more gently than it has, he has the air of someone who's opened his take-away lunch to find that it's missing dessert. They're stodgy, the pair of them, and yet between them they produced a beautiful son who made friends easily; a lazy, entitled, self-absorbed brat who thought his parents were a joke.

I think they must miss him intensely.

The woman, at least, understands that I'm here on behalf of Oksana. "Do you think Sasha harmed the Melnyk girl? Is that the drivel you're peddling?"

I start to say no, because I think they've been hurt enough, but I want to see where this goes.

"After Oksana and Sasha stopped seeing each other, she returned home with facial bruising and bleeding hands. It's possible there was a physical confrontation."

"No, no." The father's in pain, shaking his head vigorously. "You people always get it wrong. My son would never hurt anyone."

The mother is less placating. She points to the door and she's quaking with anger. "You're just another damned busy-body," she snarls.

I leave feeling chastened. I've overstepped bounds, I've crossed lines. I decide that things are best left in the hands of the detectives. This decision lasts an hour.

At home, I'm going over Sasha's texts to Misha from the Sorochintsy Fair when I come across the photo of Sasha and Oksana flanking a man in 19th century military dress. I text the photo back to Misha, asking if he knows who this person might be.

Misha texts me that the person in the photo is a soldier. Probably an old time soldier.

I call Elizaveta. She's also in the dark. Then I recall something she said previously, that Oksana was thrilled about going backstage at one of the plays. Does Elizaveta happen to recall which play? No, she says, but last year's lineup may still be online.

I thank her and ring off. It turns out the Sorochintsy Fair has its own site, and I check the offerings of the Poltava Musical Drama Theatre at the fairground for the previous summer, and find *Natalka Poltavka*, and *Moskal-Wizard*.

Moskal-Wizard lists Artëm Hovorov in the role of Mikael, the army captain who returns home to find his wife in an unorthodox relationship with a local clerk. A separate Poltava Musical Drama Theatre website carries a picture of Artëm Hovorov, which matches the man in the picture with Sasha and Oksana.

Artëm is dark haired, rough-looking, a gaping smile. It's a studio pic, but my instinct is to look him up in the cop data base, and guess what? Probation for sexual assault. Source of this info: Russian police, Sochi.

Intriguing, but does it justify going to Poltava? Dimitri's birthday is two days off and he wants me to meet him in Odessa.

I mull. Bottom line, the two teens left Kiev in high spirits. When they returned, Oksana had been battered and had suffered a personality change. Sasha, instead of going home to a mild scolding (and his computer and sound system, and his lazy cat) took a train to another country. Something happened, something drastic.

If I swap shifts with someone, I could end up getting the next three days.

At this point my mother calls me from Boryspil. She's at my grandmother's house, and she has something to discuss with me.

****

My grandmother lives in downtown Boryspil, and it's here that my mother's asked me to meet her. I park behind her building, lift a sack of plums and a box of chocolates from the passenger seat, and make a point of locking the car door. My grandmother's apartment is located in an area of homogenous apartment buildings, where the streets are lined with birch and wild chestnuts, and every block is serviced by a tiny grocery story. This particular building is more antiquated and less well tended; the pathway among the overgrown fruit trees is unpaved, the grass brown, and the walls are tagged with graffiti, most of it profane. *Glory to Ukraine!* is the most innocuous.

Born in Boryspil, I had a serene childhood, occasionally jolted by the tantrums of my father, a Public Works Official. My dad is now retired, while my mother continues teaching graphic arts at a branch of Kiev University.

I remember the elevator to be capricious, and I climb the stairs. My mother greets me with a brisk hug. It's scarcely less warm inside the apartment, but a pair of fans are whirring in the kitchen, causing the sheer curtains to flutter and flop.

I kiss my grandma and catch the aroma of something lovely baking. I find a colander to rinse the plums as my grandmother pours me tea. She dabs perspiration from her brow. She'd be cooler in shorts and a tee, but she waves off my suggestion; she's happy in a sturdy cotton number cut to mid-calf.

I fill a fruit bowl, and head into the next room to say hello to Mafalda the pug, who's been napping and is only mildly pleased to see me.   The apartment sparkles with crystal knick-knacks, everything is scented and pristine. I'm suddenly happy, I've fallen into a basket of fresh linens, I'm safe as can be, even my ancestors, tilting downward beneath the crown molding, watch over me.

When I return to the kitchen, my mother points to a chair and I sit. She wants my advice on how to break the news to Anna that she's divorcing our father. She states this matter-of-factly, as if her other daughter Katya (me) had no emotional investment. Why does she do that? How have I proven deficient in the feelings department? (Let me give you a hint. It's because I've chosen to be a cop.)

"Your sister is emotionally fragile," says my mother. Like my grandmother, she's a kind person who thinks the best of people. What she means is that Anna cries and carries on.

I roll my eyes when my mother says this. This is not the first time that my mother's made plans to divorce, and Anna throws a fit every time.

What my mom *really* wants is for me to break the news to Anna.

"I'm on a trip for a couple of days," I say, avoiding responsibility. "Oh, Katusha!" exclaims my grandmother. Both women are instantly on alert, they're certain that romance is involved, and want to be briefed. Instead I inform my mother and grandmother that I'm looking into a situation that may bear on Oksana Melnyk's murder. The mood swiftly alters, both are horrified, poor Ilya, poor Anna!

I tell them about Oksana and Sasha Yegoshin, and the clandestine trip to the Poltava Fair. I have no evidence that this is anything other than a typical teen escapade, but I sensationalize shamelessly, so that my grandmother clucks her tongue, and my mother nods knowingly.

"Break-up violence," says my mother. "Tru-Vision did a segment last month." She gets up to pull a tray from the oven.

"What kind of cookies?" I don't really need to ask; my nose works fine.

"Oatmeal," she replies. "I intended them for Anna's children, but since you're headed in the opposite direction…"

I swallow, because I'm salivating. My mother returns to the table and inspects the plums. "Anna says you're sulking over this business with your cat."

"I'm not paying her for the surgery."

My mother grimaces. "This is a little delicate, but…she borrowed the money from me." She makes a little gesture with her hands that's says, *hate to ask, but I need the money.*

Damn. I dig for my checkbook. I'm now flat broke for the trip I'm about to make. My needy, emotionally stunted, interfering family spoils everything.

Part III - Odessa

Two and a half hours later I'm in Poltava.

I now have an address for Artëm Hovorov, Captain Mikael in *Moskal-Wizard*, but no good excuse to show up asking questions. Fortunately, the truth occasionally serves as a cover story. I decide to say that Sasha Yegoshin has gone missing from his home for over a year, and I'm following up on photos and videos made by his friends.

The address is an apartment house on Cherbonoarmiis'ka; it's shortly after midday and no one's home. I leave, get a hotdog and a soda from a snack truck, and decide to head over to the Poltava Theatre, but first I return to Artëm's apartment and knock again. This time an elderly man answers, his hair is damp and slicked to his skull, and I've the feeling that maybe he was here earlier, but not fully dressed on a sultry August day.

I ask for Artëm.

Why do I want Artëm? I show the picture of Artëm with Sasha and Oksana. The old guy isn't buying it.

"My grandson's a well-known actor, hundreds of people take pictures with him," he assures me. "He's nothing to do with someone's missing brat."

"No doubt you're right, but just in case…."

Grandpa knows something is fishy, but maybe he thinks all sorts of things are fishy - the weather forecast is off, his pension check is short, maybe I'm really a cop.

I put away my phone with the photo of Artëm and discover three oatmeal cookies my mother slipped into my shoulder bag, and I take one out and hand it to him. "My mother baked these this morning," I say. Then I turn to go.

I'm at the bottom of the stair when I hear him calling down. "He's at the fair," says Grandpa. "He's the dolphin."

****

I visited Sorochintsy Fair many times as a child, Mom was keen on the arts and crafts, Anna and Slava loved the rides and food, Dad enjoyed pointing out that the fraudulent goat-hair sweaters were made in Tajikistan, not Ukraine.

I loved the amateur singing groups on the wooden stages, in embroidered blouses and traditional headdresses, and to my seven-year-old mind this was the height of rock stardom.

Today on a low wooden stage in front of a windmill a high school band is tooting its best, and circling the audience is a person in a dolphin suit, passing out handbills. I feel my brow knitting, as the dolphin is hardly taller than me, and I'm no giant.

I plant myself in his path and say "Mr. Hovorov, can you spare a moment?"

The dolphin hands me a flier for *Natalka Poltavka.*

I tap on his proboscis. "Artëm, could you come out of there?"

"I can't. I'm in character."

I'm nonplussed. "What's a dolphin's character?"

"Open to new things. Think Amsterdam."

Amsterdam makes me think of prostitutes. "What's a dolphin rapist like?"

He struggles with the dolphin head, finally wrenching it off. His face is red from confinement, and sweat runs down his jaw.

"I didn't catch that."

"I understand you received probation for sexual assault".

"Who are you?"

"You're not in any trouble. I'm looking for someone."

"Look somewhere else."

"I bet you could use a break. Can I buy you a beer?"

He's dark haired, has uneven facial scruff and a long, sloping nose and wide mouth; the turquoise irises of his eyes are ringed by black. He has the look of an ancient, authentic Ukrainian line, and I can see him in a museum painting, where he's shoeing horses, or scything hay.   We walk between the straw covered canopies that shield the vendors from the sun.

Artëm's eyeing the kabobs and roast corn, and I offer to treat before taking stock of my shrinking cash supply. He accepts, and I shell out for goat-on-a-stick, a salted cob, and two micro brews from Kharkov, and we find ourselves seats.

"I was eighteen, and sloppy drunk at the Sochi Winter Olympics," says Artëm. "I tried to kiss an Austrian slalom skier. She put me in a headlock and dropped me off her balcony. I fell two stories onto cement and broke my right ankle. Her coach pressed charges, and the Russians threw me out of the country."

"What about these two?" I show him photos of Sasha and Oksana.

"Young love," he says. *"Natalka Poltavka, without the allegory."*

"Tell me about them."

"I was driving to Odessa for a try out. They asked if they could ride along."

"How was their mood?"

"They thought everything was hysterical. Every five minutes they had to lock lips. It was cute."

"Do you remember what they talked about?"

"At that age? Stream of consciousness."

"Give it a shot. And do you mind if I try a piece?" I'm famished, but if I pay for more food I may not have gas money.

He nudges off a generous chunk of goat.

"They had a camera and microphone, and a laptop. That's how they were raising cash, logging onto an online gaming site, set up to receive donations. They talked about that."

I chew goat. I taste garlic, cumin, fennel, fresh mint. It's possibly the most delicious thing I've ever eaten. "Do you know which site?"

"Maybe Twitch. Or Gamer-Bro."

"No game console?"

"A PC works; it depends on the game."

"So you took them to Odessa."

"Nope. They planned to visit the waterpark in Kobleve, but my car broke down. It was a day-long repair, I stayed, they hitchhiked."

"Where did you break down?"

"A few kilometers north of Nikolaev."

I do a calculation, Nikolaev can't be more than an hour from the coast.   A pony with folded fabric wings and a unicorn horn is led past, and a tiny boy in the saddle radiates enchantment.

"Why a dolphin?"

Artëm reaches beneath his arm to stroke the dolphin nose. "The bear and the zebra never stop bitching."

"Hard to get into character?"

"Extremely."

I thank him for talking to me, and make my way to the fair entrance. I don't believe Artëm caused the devastation in Oksana's life; in fact, I like him. I figure that getting kicked out of Russia is a solid character reference.

That's my visit to the fair, except I stop to barter for a wide brimmed straw hat because I'm verging on serious sunburn. It turns out that a hat costs a week's salary for a cop; it seems each hat is woven by larks in a wheat field, while an orchestra plays in the hedgerow, and they're not budging on the price.

I head back to my car. I'm hot and hungry and a have a ten-hour drive ahead, and I've just wasted a trip to Poltava. There's now no point in going on to Kobleve. If Artëm had taken them all the way to the waterpark, I might know where they stayed, and someone might remember them.

Someone might know what shattered their lives.

****

I stop in Kremenchuk around 18.00 and offer my credit card for a sandwich and chips, and wait nervously while it's approved.   I check online and review the situation. There are over twenty hotels in Kobleve, and querying hotel staff about a couple of kids from a year ago is futile. I don't have official standing to ask for registration logs, although I might be permitted to look if I paid for the privilege, but as I've pointed out, I'm tight on cash.

While I'm eating I have another thought, which is the babushka rentals. In the evenings, the old ladies gather at the train stations to rent their spare rooms, and babushkas have formidable powers of recall.

I drive until midnight, passing the city of Nikolaev, and arrive in Kobleve. I'm tapped out. I pull over near the bus station. While I'm pondering where to sleep, my head droops, a woman in traditional Ukrainian costume raps on my window and asks if I care to see a herd of pink cows, and six hours later I wake up with an urgent need to pee. Fortunately, the bus station restrooms are open. It's too early to check out the babushka rentals, and I decide to head to Odessa.

***

The day heats up and drains of color, the sky pales, the air blurs. I arrive in Odessa bedraggled, sodden with perspiration, and park the car downtown on Katerynyn'ka Ave. I retrieve a rucksack from the back seat and call Dimitri.

"Oh, good, come on over. Everyone's waiting to meet you."

Instant panic attack. "Who's everyone?"

"My little sister and her husband."

I want to hang up and walk away, I've been set up. I delay and try to think of a way out. "I need to freshen up."

"You can do that here."

"I'm hot and slimy, like those lung fish they dig up in Africa."

He laughs. "You're nervous. They'll love you."

I have a choice. I have three, actually. I can head back to Kiev. I can go as I am and be mortified. Or I can spend money I don't really have on a hotel room and a shower.

"Be there in ten," I tell Dimitri.

I'm lying, I plan to bolt. I'll tell him I was called into work. In Kiev. Nine hours away.

I decide on option number four, which is a hobo's shower in the restroom at the Granat Café, and then a quick breakfast of tea and a cabbage bun, after which I walk a block and a half to the apartment of Dimitri's parents, whom, he swore to me, are at the summer Olympics in Brazil.

****

Dimitri opens the door, pulls me inside, kisses me. "Happy Birthday" I tell him.

I drop my backpack and remove my sneakers and he slides his arm around my shoulders and urges me toward the kitchen.

A young woman looks up from a cutting board and smiles and says hi. A beaming fellow with a beard and the kindest face ever, comes forward, thrusts out his hand, and says in English, "Hi, I'm Frank."

I reply with "I'm Katya, nice to meet you," the entirety of my English, which I've summoned from middle school days.

"Frank's a Jesus freak," says Dimitri. "This is my sister Lera."

Dimitri's sister is...following my gaze. "Seven months," she tells me, cupping her belly.

"Congratulations."

"Thanks. Have you had breakfast?"

I've had a cabbage roll, so I say I've eaten; I can't walk in and start shoving food in my face. And everywhere there's food. Stacks of it. Trays of it. Buckets of it.

"We have Communion this morning," says Frank, this time in Russian. "Before that we have Member's Meeting, and before that we have Fellowship, which is the purpose of the snacks."

Frank is Canadian, an evangelical, whose small church, Wings of Rapture, works with refugees from eastern Ukraine and Crimea. I know this because Dimitri described his family a few days ago, back when I thought of them in the abstract – crepe paper cut-outs, perhaps - whom I'd never need to deal with.

Abruptly Frank prepares to leave, he's off to pick up refugees from a housing project. He invites me to attend today's sermon at the church and meet other congregants; he possesses that genuine goodwill that's hard to resist. If I weren't a seasoned road cop, immune to entreaty, I might have agreed.

I ask for the bathroom, take my backpack, change out of my tee and into a real shirt. My pupils in the mirror are super large from poor sleep, my cheeks sunken from hunger and dehydration, and I don't look half bad. I return to the kitchen with renewed confidence.

I recall that Lera's a psychologist, and I ask if she works with refugees too. She tells me it's how she met Frank. "We both practice unconditional positive regard," she says with a smile.

"I hear you investigate murders in your free time," she adds.

I think of Mrs. Grojsman's assessment of my character. "I'm a busybody," I say.

She laughs. "Me too. Anything current?"

Dimitri, always the reporter, pricks up his ears. His conscience doesn't impede his search for news even if it means throwing me under a tram. I vacillate, before deciding that the current situation is different, I'm not giving away police matters if I describe my efforts to follow an ice-cold trail - I may as well be investigating the Rasputin murder. I open the photo app on Oksana's IPhone.

Lera studies a shot of Oksana, and shakes her head sadly. "Pretty girl!" She passes it to Dimitri. "The other, the boyfriend? Can't you put out a bulletin?"

"For the moment he's not a suspect," I say.

"What's your instinct telling you?"

I describe Oksana's bruising, abrasions, and subsequent personality disintegration. "It could be a violent break-up," I conclude. "It explains why Oksana went into a tailspin, and why Sasha went on the lam."

"Maybe they committed a crime," says Lara, briskly swathing a plate of pickled mushrooms in food wrap. "They needed money and held up a grocery store."

"It's possible."

"Or perhaps both were the victims of an attack. Did the boy have injuries?"

"No one knows. He turned up in Minsk shortly after, in his usual high spirits."

"Where were they last seen?" asks Dimitri.

I slip my arm around his waist. "North of Nikolaev, by an actor who was driving them to Odessa, but had car trouble."

"Was the girl injured at that point?"

"No."

"Check the news for August of last year," suggests Dimitri. "Odessa and Kobleve area."

Dimitri brings a laptop, and we sift through last August's local news. Dimitri bookmarks possibilities. A hit and run, the man charged was local. A robbery in Odessa, man shot by police. Multiple reports of vandalism and thievery.

Nothing seems to have bearing on the fate of the two teens.

"Maybe it's not what, but who?" says Lera. "They offended someone, and were threatened, or beaten. It's easy to say the wrong thing these days."

"Can't you contact the Yegoshin boy?" asks Dimitri.

"He's been sending texts from Minsk," I say, "but won't pick up his phone."

"You're sure he's there? Any photos?"

I scroll through photos and find Sasha in front of the cascade fountain. Lera studies it briefly and passes it to Dimitri.

"It's been photo-shopped." he says. "It's a fake."

***

Frank's pastel-blue church is a minimalist operation, with pews, wooden cross and podium on the first floor, plus a jumble of boxes containing donated clothing. From Lera's van we convey baskets of food down a stairway into a cool basement where tables are draped with embroidered cloths.

I don't know precise numbers on Ukrainian refugees, but over a million have fled from the fighting in the east, and refugees from Crimea add to the crisis. They need food and clothing, plus jobs, housing, health care, and in many cases counseling, and most of the aid comes not from our government, which is broke, but from private groups like Frank's.

As soon as we finish setting out trays of food, Lera says, "If you two were hoping to spend time together, now's the time to make a dash for it. Once my husband arrives, you'll be pressed into service for the rest of the afternoon."

****

The Burger Club adjoins the Dolphinarium, there are palm trees and geyser fountains on the plaza, and the Black Sea is a few meters distant.

We both order burgers and beers, and eat outside.

"I have an idea about your mystery," Dimitri tells me. He lays it out. Inside my head pieces of a puzzle fall into place, and the obvious emerges.

"I've got to make a call," I say. Reluctantly I set aside my bacon burger, wipe my fingers, and phone Ivan Rudskoy.

"Oksana Melnyk had a boyfriend, Sasha Yegoshin," I inform him.

"We know. He's in Belarus."

"He may be closer to home," I say. "Can you round up a cadaver-sniffing dog?"

****

The sun is setting when we return to the apartment, and not long after, Lera and Frank show up with a birthday cake.

Obligatorily there's a certain amount of alcohol consumed at birthday bashes, except by Frank, who abstains. It's a modest celebration for a famous TV personality, but Dimitri seems content. I find my backpack and pull out a framed print from Dimitri's playing days with the Dynamos. "Happy thirtieth," I say.

He grins. "You figured I wanted a picture of myself? Is that a hint?"

"Nope. I've had it on my mantelpiece since puberty, twined in twinkly lights."

"You haven't got a mantelpiece." He studies the picture. "Anyway, you're not getting it back. I look too damn good."

Two hours later we are left alone, and things turn romantic. (You're in luck because I'm going to spare you and skip ahead.)

The phone rings. The call is from Ivan Rudskoy. "A body's been found."

In the older, disused side of the junkyard, near a stack of preformed slabs, overgrown by weeds and covered by a cement slab, a shallow grave has been carefully excavated.

"How many people to place the slab?"

"Three, four. There's another possibility, which is that a cement slab was already leaning against a stack, and they chose that spot because they could tip it over to conceal the grave."

"How many people in the second scenario?"

"We're talking a hundred kilos. At least two, maybe three."

"Is it Sasha Yegoshin?"

"It's not *not* him. We're waiting to see." He pauses. "Oksana Melnyk knew he was there."

"Or the person who killed her, knew he was there."

I can hear him snort. He prefers his own version. "Lots of Tru-Vision people at the Crane Graveyard," he adds. "I didn't call them."

"Me neither," I say.

****

Back in Kiev, Monday night shift. I'm dispatched to the train station just before midnight because a dog has been abandoned and someone is injured. I find an overwrought albino mastiff, short-chained to the hand rail in the disabled stall of the women's bathroom, howling and slavering, it's neck bleeding from frenzied efforts to free itself. A girl in a wheelchair has fractured her hip, after being obliged to use a regular stall, and is being borne away on a stretcher.

A floral crown is shredded on the stall floor, and I believe the dog was wearing it.

I'm on my own. Animal control has its hands full with a trailer of swine that's overturned on the Patona Bridge; there are dead swine, rampaging swine, and swine swimming in the Dneiper.

Within minutes of my arrival three women in party dresses enter, and a fourth in a wedding gown; all are dipso, and all wear floral crowns. I've let out slack on the mastiff's chain, and he makes a tail-wagging beeline for the bride. I ask for an explanation.

It turns out that the bride's family boycotted the wedding; she arrived solo from Lvov on the noon train, and couldn't persuade a taxi driver to chauffeur the mastiff to church. She parked the dog in the bathroom.

The groom pops his head in, and discovers that his new wife chained a frantic dog in the train station for twelve hours. His reaction is sheer dismay. Drunk as he is, he's aware that he's married a woman who's devoid of basic human feelings. Additionally, there may be criminal charges because of the injured wheelchair girl, so I cuff the bride and haul her to HQ.

The dog opts for a train trip to the honeymoon suite at Koruna Mountain. So does the groom.

****

The search is on for Sasha Yegoshin's phone, and for the person who was texting fake pictures of Sasha in Minsk to his classmates. Oksana's room is searched by detectives, as is Misha Grojsman's. No luck.

That leaves one person, but I'm keeping mum. I'll give you a hint. Her first name is Elizaveta, Oksana's best friend. The question I'm asking myself is, why?

****

As for my meddling in the Oksana Melnyk murder case, the detectives pretend to believe my tip on Sasha Yegoshin was pure guesswork. They know it wasn't, and I expect soon I'll be summoned to Commander Shulikov's office. Meanwhile, I ask Ruslan Omelechko, the medical examiner's intern, if I can take a look at Sasha's body. Ruslan says no, and complains that my requests are jeopardizing his job.

Ruslan and I are like ricocheting billiard balls, sometimes we experience direct impact (always at his place) but I've been neglecting him since meeting Dimitri, so I don't push it. I say I'm interested in knowing how the body was buried, whether with care, by someone who knew him, or shoved into the dirt, by someone who didn't.

"He was barefoot, but otherwise fully clothed. No bones were broken, and no roses were thrown in last minute." His voice is crisp, even snippy.

"You've been helpful, thanks."

"No problem." He hangs up on me.

****

I sleep all day, wake about 19.00 and eat a yoghurt. I brew tea. I'm thinking about the news stories that Dimitri dug up from last August, and a phrase from a hit and run report echoes persistently in my head: "local man charged." I decide to check out whether the local man was convicted. That's where it gets interesting.

In May a car was towed from a Kiev parking garage, where its prepaid space had expired. An officer ran the plates and notified a music teacher in Nikolaev that his stolen Moskvitch has been located. A flag popped up. A hit and run in Nikolaev, involving a vehicle of similar description, had occurred the same week that the car was stolen. Testing on the Moskvitch revealed blood on a cracked headlight. The music teacher, Boris Shemetov, was questioned, and claimed he was at a teachers' conference in Kiev, which witnesses corroborated.

That left Boris' travel day to Kiev. Also the day of the accident.

It was possible, and seemed increasingly likely to the investigators, that Boris Shemetov had run down the victim, and then driven the Moskvitch to Kiev where he parked it. Shemetov was arrested and jailed, and when the blood on the headlight was confirmed as the victim's, he was also suspended from his job as music teacher. Community outrage boiled over.

This is why:

The casualty was a staunch seventy-four-year-old caregiver who made the rounds of Nikolaev on her bicycle, bringing the bedridden and elderly their prescription meds, and assisting with bathing and light housecleaning. Whenever she couldn't manage herself, she found someone who could. Her name was Agafa Torokhtiy.

In short, a saint. A saint who survived six agonizing hours with a shattered pelvis and ruptured spleen after being struck down.

Photos show a woman in a scarf, a brown, shapeless sack of a dress, orange sneakers, arms draped with bags of supplies.

I may be the only person who doesn't believe Boris Shemetov mowed down Agafa and left her for dead.

I think Sasha Yegoshin did it.

****

Anna is moping. We're not speaking, but we're not quarreling, either. Our parents, on whom she's patterned her life, are divorcing, and I'm guessing she's having an existential moment or two as she sorts the day's third load of laundry. If you think I'm feeling smug (me, the contrary daughter who joined the police force) you're not wrong.

I rise at four AM and point the Volga toward Nikolaev, home of music teacher Boris Shemetov.

School # 19 in Nikolaev is adjacent to the city's train station. If Oksana and Sasha hitchhiked to Nikolaev, they may have asked to be dropped off here. I could easily be wrong. Maybe they hitched all the way to Kobleve. A spatter of rain clears off soon after I arrive in the city. I park and check out the train station. The bathrooms are open and functional. I don't know if they were open on the day of the hit and run last year, but it may be important. It could be a reason to cross the street and duck through the hedge onto the school grounds.

I leave the station, cross over, find a well-traveled route through the hemlock shrubs, and begin searching for the parking area where Boris Shemetov left his Moskvitch. There are spaces immediately behind the school, in more than one location, but nothing that appears to be the main lot. I'm undecided. The marked spaces behind the school aren't visible from the street, at least not from the station. If Oksana and Sasha wandered over, it was likely for some other purpose than car theft. Maybe privacy, or perhaps shade from the heat, or to have a pee.

I don't see Oksana and Sasha as experienced car thieves, but no worries, according to the police report, the owner left the keys on the dash under a pair of sunglasses. His wife was picking up the car later in the day.

I traverse the campus and emerge at the main entrance. As I circle back to my car, I pass a mini-mart and pop in for an energy drink. I also browse the freezer novelties and choose an ice cream bar. In the car I'm lapping away like a contented cat, when a section of the wrapper catches my eye.

Distributed by Grojsman Inc., Kiev.

Misha Grojsman? His dad owns Grojsman Inc.? The name is a coincidence? I think about it, but it doesn't seem to fit anywhere.

I wipe my fingers, and call the number I have for Agafa Torokhtiy. A woman answers. I say I'm with the Kiev police (I don't say in what capacity) and ask If I can drop by.

I drive from the school to the home of Agafa Torokhtiy. If the car thieves were heading for Kobleve, the most direct route would be to head for E58 west. Agafa's house lies on that route.

There was a witness to the accident, or its immediate aftermath, but the details are sketchy.

The Torokhtiy place, home of the late Agafa Torokhtiy, is enclosed by street walls, but the gate has been left unlatched. Swaying purple lavender chokes the walkway, and white roses dance in a stiffening breeze.

Natasha Torokhtiy turns out to be well-spoken, refined in manner, early forties. She's attractively attired in a low cut white blouse and dark skirt. A silver necklace with a bright blue stone hangs between breasts that could best be described as generous, humungous, or acutely in need of reduction surgery.

I understand she's the victim's daughter-in-law, there's no husband in evidence, and I don't inquire. The house bears the stamp of an older generation, there's a single row of icons on the wall above the divan, and unlit candles cluster on a corner table, and tapestry cloths are spread on chair backs. An ancient, emaciated little dog stares in my direction with blind eyes. I feel I'm in a Turgenev novel, and any minute the steward will come in to give an accounting of the harvest. The house smells overpoweringly of lavender; I think the lady's boiling some sprigs on the stove to freshen the air. It's a bit much.

Natasha Torokhtiy doesn't find it odd that I've shown up, and she's expecting to hear there've been developments in the case.

"I told them I'd seen a red Lada with patched fender. I was mistaken, I was informed later that the car in question was a Moskvitch. I'm afraid I'm no expert. My uncle had a Lada, that's what I thought it was.

"I'd gone out with her and opened the gate. Aggie was overloaded as always, but that day it was worse. She was wobbling, the bike was actually weaving along the road from being overbalanced."

She sneaks a look at me. "I didn't tell the police that part. Are you going to report me?"

"No."

"I didn't want them to think the accident was Agafa's fault, because it wasn't."

"I understand."

"I turned back when the car flew past. I ran down the street toward them, the car reversed, and someone looked out the window at my mother, then saw me, I suppose. They started up, and quickly accelerated. A few seconds later they turned the corner."

"You saw the driver?"

"Only a blur. I'm useless without my glasses."

Natasha makes a face. "Agafa was defenseless on that old bike. I warned her. I said one day she'd be squashed in the road like a garden toad."

She swivels on the divan and points to a shelf of photos. "That's her."

In one portrait, a gap-toothed girl of six or seven presses her face firmly against the old lady's. "That's Savina, my baby."

"You ran into my gran recently. We all know how that turned out."

"How old is Savina?" I ask conversationally.

"Well, six in this picture, I think, but that was eons ago. She'll be thirteen in October."

My mystery caller, revealed at last.

On the shelf above the photographs stands a row of children's books, and the back cover of the nearest bears Natasha Torokhtiy's photograph. "You wrote these?" I ask.

"Oh, yes. My other children." She sighs.

It seems Mrs. Torokhtiy is a writer. I've never heard of her, but I don't read children's books. I tend to read the books my sister Anna purchases at the news kiosk, which are billed as romances, but are mainly erotica.

"Aggie never got angry, you know. I couldn't have asked for a kinder mother-in-law. She loved the garden. I planted it again this year."

She guides me through the kitchen and mudroom into the back yard, where the ground cover is a tangle of yellowing late-summer vines. A white cat lounges on a blue bench, and beside the bench gourds and squashes of varying sizes and colors are stacked. Mrs. Torokhtiy picks her way through the garden. The breeze rings an iron wind chime at the corner of the house; the result is more cow bell than chime.

She thrusts aside stalks to reveal a monstrosity, a giant orange-white squash thing; a pumpkin, or a freak of nature. She squats and settles on it, glances up to see if I get it. "Cinderella, going to the ball," she tells me.

Not addled, just a middle-aged woman enjoying a moment of levity. The chime sounds again.

I lend her a hand up. "It's damp," she says happily. She swipes a spider web from her arm and laughs self-consciously. "A good tale always has spiders – and a moldy underside, and lurking unknowns."

"Princes who turn into toads."

She smiles. "You're too young to be cynical," she admonishes.

Part IV - Boris

I'm curious to find out whether the thieves left personal effects in the car.

Located in a closely packed neighborhood of single family residences, the house of Boris Shemetov, the Moskvitch owner, is fronted by a street wall of crumbling blue plaster. A metal grate, overgrown by a vine, allows a glimpse of the house, and the metal door in the wall is locked. I ring the bell. Between the outside wall and the street pavement a row of pepper plants has been recently watered.

After several minutes a woman emerges and appraises me through the grate. "Yes?"

"I'm with the Kiev police," I tell her. "I'm inquiring about the stolen Moskvitch."

The bolt slides; a petite redhead looks up at me. She's in a white T-top that doesn't conceal, in fact emphasizes, a strawberry birthmark covering most of her right shoulder and arm. She eyes me with suspicion, and the corner of her mouth twists wryly.

"My husband's not here."

My first thought is that's he's in jail. I'm confused. "I understand the charges were dropped."

"Oh yes." She titters, there's vindication in her expression. "One of his girlfriends."

"Pardon?"

She plays with the dead bolt, sliding it back and forth. "Miss Levshenko, who teaches geometry at his school, vouched for the missing hours in his alibi."

"I see." Although I don't.

"At the time of the accident she was in a bathroom on the train to Kiev."

"Yes?"

"My husband was lending her a hand. Or a finger."

Sometimes I'm really thick, but finally I catch on.

There's a cry of distress through the open door, and *"Mama!"*

"I have to go," she tells me.

"Your husband?"

"Moved out. He's at his father's place west of town, in Vesnyane.   Ask for the bee farm."

She closes the gate and I hear the bolt snick into place. In the car I jot down details of the alibi - *Levshenko, geometry*. I'm heartened to learn math is involved; perhaps things will add up.

I cross a bridge, soon find a wooden sign depicting a bee in flight, and pull into a long drive with poplars, and beyond them, mowed fields dotted with bales of hay. At the end of the lane sits an ancient brown house, with white and blue gingerbread windows, and a corrugated tin roof. A silver samovar sits on a picnic table, and beside it lie branches of willow herb and briar rose.

I leave the car and continue on foot along the lane. A man is at work in a pear orchard, where as many as thirty box-hives with supers, painted in flower colors, are staggered in rows. The fruit on the trees is green, the trees are ringed by buckwheat that's now seeded. I have a phobia of bees and wasps and in my mind they're one and the same; among stinging insects there are no good guys.

The bee keeper catches sight of me, and turns. I approach as closely as I dare. He lifts the protective netting over his hat, and then, perhaps out of courtesy, removes his hat as well, even though the bees fill the air around us. His close-cropped hair is grizzled - this is not Boris Shemetov.

He nods toward the Volga. "She's a beauty. I see you take care of her."

"Not me. My dad." I can't imagine how he's determined the condition of the old Volga from this distance, but I assume he's being congenial. My throat has contracted as the drone of bees intensifies, and my voice is squeaky with suppressed alarm.

He's wielding a peculiar contraption, a tea-kettle type of apparatus with a small bellows attached at the back. He catches the direction of my glance, and squeezes the bellows, causing pine scented smoke to jet from the upturned spout. "A smoker, to calm the bees."

He looks me over. "You haven't respected the summer sun," he reprimands. "Try potato juice next time."

"I'll remember," I promise. My arms are peeling after my exposure the previous week, and I bear more than a slight resemblance to a molting bird.

"I was hoping to speak to Boris Shemetov," I say. "I'm with Kiev police. I may have an idea who stole his car."

I follow him back along a path into a garden, where rows of flowers and vegetables alternate. As soon as we're out of range of the hives I relax.

"My son's making a delivery," he says. He places the bee smoker atop a shelf on the outside wall of the house, near a box of pine needles. "Here he is now." I hear the distinctive racket of a single cylinder engine, and see a man approaching along the lane on a moped, a wire basket behind his seat.

My companion waits as his son reaches the house. "You have a visitor from the Kiev police," he tells Boris. He winks at me. "A pretty one."

Boris does not respond, barely glances my way. He dismounts and wheels the moped inside the open garage.

The father shrugs, offers me his hand, and then strides away toward the hives.

"I've read the report you made to the police," I tell Boris the music teacher. He doesn't respond.

Maybe I'm being too brusque. I attempt a conversational approach. "Only a week 'till classes resume. Are you looking forward?"

"I lost my job," he says bluntly.

"Was that related to the hit and run?"

"What do you think?" he snaps.

Boris is a tall, twenty-something fellow in denim shorts, sneakers, tee. By tall I mean: 1.9, easy. His face is nicely proportioned, light brown hair, eyes grey and widely spaced, but there's a yellow cast to his teeth, and he needs a haircut and shave.

"May I see the car?"

I'm led through the garage, which is cluttered with auto parts, and bee-keeping paraphernalia, and exit a rear door before descending a set of bowed wooden steps. The Moskvitch, a boxy, dark red vehicle, with a mismatched grey fender, is parked in a patch of wildflowers, where chick weed and golden rod have hedged it in.

"That's it."

"You stopped driving it."

"Wouldn't you? I can't even sell it; the gears are stripped. Whoever stole it couldn't manage a standard transmission."

I indicate the fender. "Was this damaged in the hit and run?"

"No, Miss, that's an old patch."

He points out a headlight. "This was smashed. Still had blood on it when the police sent it back."

"Did the thieves leave anything behind?"

"Trash. Candy wrappers and an empty soda can. The police found fingerprints, but no matches. Also a cash receipt for aspirin from the Vitalux Pharmacy."

"The Vitalux in Nikolaev?"

"No. Kobleve."

"Do you still have the receipt?"

His gaze shifts away. "I tossed it out with the rest."

He's lying, but I move on. "You said in the report that you'd left the keys in the car, and the doors were unlocked."

"I explained all that. My wife was picking up the car. We'd arranged she'd drop me off, but we argued that morning. I took the car and told her I'd leave it at the school."

"She didn't report the car stolen when she came for it?"

"She didn't realize. She never left to pick it up." He moves toward the rear entrance of the house and I tag along. "Have you found out who's responsible?" he asks. His eyes say he has little hope that a police officer will be forthcoming.

"No. I'm trying to eliminate a possibility."

He believes I'm obfuscating. "I don't want revenge," he says. "I just want them to know how much harm they did."

He catches himself. "I mean besides the doctor." I believe he means old Agafa, who wasn't a doctor, but a caregiver. He looks embarrassed. "I won't go into it, but proving it wasn't me was a nightmare, and the whole thing was expensive."

"I'm very sorry," I tell him.

"There are people who still suspect me," he adds. "I couldn't account for the day of the accident. In fact, I was on the train, but I couldn't prove it in the beginning, except to say I didn't magically teleport to Kiev, did I? What the devil did they think?"

His look of injustice is raw.

I remember what his wife told me about the restroom shenanigans, and I think he doesn't need to look so outraged.

****

Monday. I'm back in Kiev, and back at work. A man has thrown himself from the twenty-eighth floor of Gazprom, and I'm diverting traffic while the body is removed. Tru-Vision arrives, and Dimitri Nikolayev sprints over with a camera and we pretend we don't know each other, while I tell him I have no information on the victim or why he jumped. He pretends this is highly relevant. When he shuts down the camera he invites me to *Très Française* on Friday night and I accept.

Afterwards I go for tea and a cherry bar at the Blue Cup Café. While I'm between bites, I call my brother-in-law Ilya to ask if he knows whether the controls on a fork lift would be similar to a pick-and-carry crane.

"There are different types of mini-cranes," Ilya states, "but ten minutes of training will make anyone minimally proficient."

I cruise over to the warehouse of Grojsman, Ltd., where I sit and watch forklifts transport pallets onto a loading dock. Eventually I finish my tea, and climb out. I'm in uniform, and there are curious glances as I mount steps onto the apron, and slip through a plastic strip curtain into a refrigerated warehouse.

I find two men loading a pallet from a conveyer belt.

"Morning. Where would I find Mihael Grojsman?"

"Mihael who?" The fellow reaches to switch off the belt.

"The owner's son."

The second man speaks up. "He rob a candy store?"

"It's about his application to the police academy. You haven't seen him today?"

"Not likely."

 "He's young to be a cop."

"He's listed his job experience as forklift driver," I say, riffling through my notebook.

"Experience is a relative thing, isn't it?" He points to a wall where the plywood is punctured and splintered.

I adopt a severe expression. "Would that be Mr. Grojsman's handiwork?"

"Not for me to say, Miss."

"Thank you for your time."

****

When I return to my car I receive a phone call from Detective Ivan Rudskoy. He tells me the blue Mini-Cooper's been located, or at least a strong contender. A rental car was taken out of service because of leaking transmission fuel, and has been waiting for a patch at VIP-U-Rent, until Mister Rudskoy had it towed to HQ.

"Who's on the rental agreement?"

"Leysa Barkalov. Sound familiar?"

"Not remotely."

"Mrs. Barkalov, age 67, lost her eyesight in an accident four years ago and hasn't driven since. She lives in Voskresenka, and misplaced her license recently."

"Anything else?"

 "The car's being dusted for fingerprints as we speak."

"Can I take a look?"

"For what purpose, Miss Kondrashov?"

"Just because."

"Give me something from your end."

"Okay, but it's thin, and you need to come at it on tiptoe," I warn.

"You know me."

"A kid named Mihael Grojsman. His father operates Grojsman's Distribution, for frozen dairy products. Do you know what a mini-crane is?"

"Like a big crane, only smaller?"

"One type is known as a pick-and-carry. There's one at the Crane Graveyard, and my information is that it's not that tough to operate."

"There's a point here, right?"

"Misha Grojsman was Sasha Yegoshin's friend," I continue. "By extension, a friend of Oksana. It's possible he knows how to operate a forklift, and probably a mini-crane."

"You think he put the slab on the dead boy."

"I don't know, but you could ask. His daddy may pull strings if you're not nice."

"Got it."

I stop off at Domashnyaya Kuhnya for sausage soup, complemented by a side of dumplings with blueberries and cottage cheese. I order tea instead of coke, mindful of the weight I've gained recently.

I'm hoping they find evidence in the Mini Cooper. The fingerprints of Boris Shemetov will be on record. Natasha Torokhtiy isn't high on my list of suspects, but if she swiped pantyhose at her local mini-mart she may be in the system. We'll see.

After a slice of apple cake, I head to HQ for a look at the Mini Cooper. It's parked in a corner of the garage, on a sheet of plastic, and no one's working on it. I find a tech in the office.

"Anything on the Mini-Cooper?"

"It's been wiped," he tells me. "And vacuumed."

Someone had a guilty conscience. "Can I take a quick peek?"

"Nothing to see."

"I'm not looking for anything."

I open the car door and slide onto the driver's seat, close the door. Close my eyes. Inhale, exhale.

What I smell isn't lavender (Natasha Torokhtiy), nor burnt pine needles (Boris Shemetov).

It's something else, faint and elusive. I was treated to a whiff recently, but right now my nose is sending a wholly spurious memo to my brain.

It's the cologne my brother-in-law Ilya was wearing the night Oksana was killed.

Part V – Secret Ceremony

When the detectives reach Misha Grojsman's house he's ducked out. "We made the mistake of calling ahead," Mister Rudskoy tells me.

"It was a long shot, anyway," I say.

I swing by the Natalka Park amusement arcade, where I recognize one of Misha's friends from my previous visit. Today he's playing skee-ball. I advise him that abetting a felon is good for jail time. He tells me that Misha's hiding from the cops at the Cinema Deluxe.

It's a weekday afternoon; I scan the offerings at the Cinema and choose the one requiring the fewest brain cells, which is a virtual toss-up. In theater four, eight people are scattered over a sizeable auditorium of plush cream-tan seats. Misha Grojsman isn't exactly hiding, although he's partially concealed by a giant tub of popcorn. He startles as I plunk down beside him.

"I'm guessing you know how to operate a pick-and-carry crane, Misha."

He hugs his popcorn and stares at the screen, where a rhino wearing an ammo belt is pursuing giant turtles. "Am I going to prison?"

"I don't think so. Is that what you're worried about?"

His entire body contracts and he slides a few millimeters further down in his seat. "They'll annihilate me in prison."

"You're not in trouble unless you're concealing a crime, Misha. Why don't you start by telling me how Sasha died?"

Misha spends a minute considering the question.

"He drowned. He wasn't a good swimmer."

"Where?"

"In the Black Sea, in Kobleve."

"Oksana brought him back to Kiev?"

"Yeah."

"Why not call the police?"

"She freaked. They caused an accident, they stole somebody's car and hit an old woman on a bike."

Three girls in front of us suddenly get up and move.

"Why don't we adjourn to the lobby?" I suggest.

"I'll miss the end of the movie!"

"Can't be helped." We don't go to the lobby, instead we head out into the mall until I find a bench. I point and he sits.

"Did Oksana injure her face in the accident?"

"I guess. I didn't ask."

According to Misha, Oksana and Sasha arrived in Kobleve in dire need of a safe haven. Sasha, even more than Oksana, agonized over what they'd done. According to Oksana, he shut down.

"They ditched the Moskvitch behind an apartment block, Oksana rented a room, and for a few hours they hunkered down. Eventually Oksana went out for sodas and snacks, and when she got back she started playing on Sasha's gamer account. Only no one was donating."

"Where did they rent a room?"

"At a hotel, I guess."

I release a pent up breath. "Okay, just keep going."

The next morning Sasha awoke cheerfully, with no apparent memory of what had occurred the previous day, and strolled down the hallway to the bathroom. Several minutes passed before he returned, face livid. He erupted in a psychotic rant, hurling blame at the old woman, and at the idiotic Moskvitch owner, but principally at Oksana, whose responsibility as someone who cared about him was to dissuade him from doing stupid things. The tirade was followed by an intense, wrenching, crying jag.

Then, silence. Once more he curled up on the bed.

Check-out time. Out-of-money time. Oksana persuaded Sasha to go down to the beach, where they mingled dispiritedly with vacationers, sharing a bottle of water.

At noon Oksana called Elizaveta and begged her to wire money via Yandex. Elizaveta agreed, but needed time. As the afternoon advanced, Oksana made plans to spend the second night on the beach as far from the aqua park activities as possible.

"She tried to convince Sasha that they could go on as before. They'd board a train and return to Kiev, their crime undetected. They'd accidentally ended a stranger's life; they'd been unlucky, but they weren't bad people."

Slowly, Sasha seemed to come around.

"She fell asleep on the sand, and awoke to rain beating down; night had fallen and the beach had emptied. Sasha had vanished. She freaked, went looking for the car, and found it behind the apartment block where they'd parked it. Still no sign of Sasha. She ran back to the beach and starting calling out. Finally, she saw a patch of white beyond the breaking waves, and as Sasha had been wearing a white t-shirt, she was terrified it might be him."

Oksana waded into the sea until the waves were rolling over her head. Sasha floated face down in roiling surf. Exhausted and in panic mode, she struggled back to shallower water, rested, then returned to pull him in. It was too late to attempt CPR, and she was afraid to call police. She couldn't leave Sasha on the beach, either.

"That's when she lost it entirely."

She dragged Sasha's body across the beach, and lay him down beside a refreshments kiosk. Next she returned to the apartment building for the Moskvitch. She maneuvered Sasha onto the rear seat, concealed him with sheets of piano music from the glove compartment, and drove north, terrified that she'd be pulled over by police. Mid-morning, near the Nature Park outside Kiev, the Moskvitch's ill-used transmission seized up, leaving her stranded near the entrance to the carnival attractions. She phoned Misha and Elizaveta in a condition of hysterical breakdown, recounting to each, in choking breaths, an unbelievable sequence of misfortunes. In the end Misha took a cab to the park.

"Sand was on everything, on her clothes and on the car seats. I asked her to climb out, and she walked away and collapsed beside a jogging path. I wanted to have a look at Sasha, because it could have been a prank. It was the sort of elaborate joke he enjoyed contriving.

"She'd covered him with pages of music, only the pages weren't very big, and some of them had slipped off. I had to lift his head up. I thought he might start laughing, only he didn't. He was definitely dead, sand was sticking to one of his eyeballs and his skin was grey. A fluid had dried on his face, pinkish froth that must have leaked from his mouth. I took off my windbreaker and lay it over him.

"Oksana wouldn't get back in the car. I yelled at her but she kept shaking her head. Finally, she started crying and got in."

Misha climbed behind the wheel, succeeded in shifting the car into gear, and coaxed it as far as the ferry terminal, where he parked it with Sasha inside. There the Moskvitch and its lone passenger waited for the length of a hot August day. At night, the three, including Elizaveta, made the decision to bury Sasha's body at the Crane Graveyard.

"The gate was locked, but there was space to wriggle under. We lifted Sasha out of the car, I slid under the gate, and Oksana and Elizaveta pushed from their side while I pulled. Sasha kept getting snagged, but in the end he was through, and the girls followed. We carried him until Oksana got tired, and then Elizaveta and I each grabbed a foot, and we dragged him to the far wall.

"I returned for the shovel. Getting rid of the body was taking a lot of time, and I was already jittery. I started thinking I might go to jail."

Once Sasha had been buried, Elizaveta suggested using the junkyard's mini-crane to place a cement panel atop the grave.

"It was nuts, because the noise would attract attention, but that's what Oksana wanted. That's what she said we had to do. No one must ever find him, or she'd be blamed for his death, and for the death of the old lady."

I rise and pull out my phone. "Don't move," I tell Misha.

"Can I get a Cinnabon?"

"No."

I call Rudskoy. "Misha Grojsman's at the Ocean Plaza Mall. I'll keep him company until you arrive."

"Has he said anything?"

"He says Sasha Yegoshin drowned in Kobleve, and he helped bury the body."

****

Another weekend, another foray into the southern regions. I'm forced to renege on my dinner date at *Très Française*, and the phone conversation with Dimitri is bumpy. He doesn't hide that he's unhappy, but the next time he'll be less upset, and after that there won't be a next time. I believe that's what I'm waiting for, so I can return to being every-day Katya, who's not dating a TV personality.

I try to remember when I stopped being up to the challenge of dating a wonderful guy. I think it was in Odessa, when for the first time we spent an entire day together, and he didn't disappoint, and didn't turn into a frog. I couldn't handle it.

I don't have an explanation for why I'm so pathetic. Maybe I don't want to be in love. Maybe there's a wrench in Katya's emotional works.

I drive straight to Kobleve on the coast, make it in eight hours, and before doing anything else I rent a room on the beach, have a shower, and change into shorts and a tee shirt.

While I'm checking the view from my window, Lydia Melnyk calls. She's discovered that Oksana used an Instagram account, separate from her iPhone photo cache, which I've already scanned. Also, Lydia's seen the reports of Sasha Yegoshin's body being dug up at the Crane Graveyard. Have I learned anything?

"They took a road trip." I tell her what I know about the accident, and Sasha's death, and the chaotic aftermath that ended with Sasha's friends burying him in a junk yard.

"I'm no closer to learning why Oksana went to the Crane Graveyard two weeks ago," I finish.

There's an interruption on Lydia's end, I believe she's weeping. I wait, watching the action on the beach through an open window. A rubber banana boat bucks over the waves as its occupants cling to straps and shriek. More moments pass before Lydia's back. "You must have an idea," she pleads.

I tell her I'll call her as soon as I'm back in Kiev.

It's true that I haven't a clue. I don't even have possibilities. Here's why. If Oksana's murder was related to the hit and run, I'm going to have to demonstrate that either Boris Shemetov, or Natasha Torokhtiy, was able to track down the thieves when the police couldn't.

I peruse Oksana's Instagram account, and realize that all posts were made before the events of last summer. Next I search for Sasha Yegoshin on Instagram, where I soon locate the picture of him that's later been altered for a fake Minsk photo. I click on a link to his Gamer-Bro account, which is inactive, but I find an archive of previous sessions.

The final video is dated the same evening as the day of the accident. Sasha isn't playing, instead Oksana is manning the keyboard on a game called Slither. Her face is bruised, and her jaw appears swollen, although the light is murky. The room behind is partially visible, and a boy I assume is Sasha lies face down on a bunk, unmoving. Half way through the game another young man comes in, uninvited, and stands behind Oksana observing the game. For a second I think it must be Misha Grojsman, but as he bends his head to the monitor light I realize I'm mistaken. Another friend of Sasha? Oksana doesn't react to his presence; initially it's not even clear that she knows he's there and I'm half expecting her to startle.

Oksana rises, brushes past the new kid, and settles on the bunk beside Sasha. The new arrival takes over. There's a running total of donations, but very little cash is coming in, and after twenty minutes the boy switches off. Neither Oksana nor Sasha has stirred.

It's sad and strange. I have the impression that Oksana and Sasha are in a state of suspended dread, waiting for the world to end.

****

I go looking for the Vitalux Pharmacy.

Why check out the Vitalux Pharmacy, you ask? Mostly because Boris couldn't show me the receipt he found in the Moskvitch, which makes me thinks it's significant, and I'm wondering if the two teens found lodging nearby.

The Vitalux Pharmacy is three blocks from the beach and easily located. I enter, buy antacid, soda, earplugs, and Vitamin C. As I emerge I pop a chewable tablet and stand in the shade of a locust tree while it sinks in that I've accomplished nothing by coming here. I decide I may as well join the vacationers on the beach. I walk half a block, twirling my little plastic sack, and then I stop. I've paused under an awning with a banner that reads Black Sea Hostel.

My phone rings, Lydia Melnyk has learned of a troubling development.

"It's Elizaveta, Oksana's friend."

"What happened?"

"She tried to hurt herself."

"How bad?"

"She slashed herself, but she's going to survive. This is related, isn't it?"

"I don't know."

I'm shaken. I walk down to the shore, past a water slide that jettisons screaming children into the sea. The banana boat revs and leaves its mooring with another group of teens. A parasail, blue and yellow, is towed past, and I clear my mind, watching it soar, blocking out everything else. I want there to be nothing on my mind, nothing other than colored fabric floating aloft above the sea.

Instead, I think that Elizaveta has been keeping secrets. What didn't she tell me?

I loiter until sundown, then walk back. I've nearly forgotten about the Black Sea Hostel until I pass under the awning again. I climb the steps. A queue has formed at reception, and the clink of dishware issues from a cafeteria off the lobby. I read postings on a large blackboard by people requesting rides to various destinations, foreign and domestic, and several are planning to visit Crimea, recently stolen from us by the Russians.

I show my badge at the desk and ask to see the registry from last August. I'm a Kiev road cop outside my jurisdiction and I'm committing an infraction, but the girl at the desk seems unruffled. I ask her to bring up the day of the accident. All ID's have been photocopied, and I quickly find Alexander Yegoshin. Sasha's name is among eight others who checked in that evening.

Beneath Sasha's ID, I find Katya Kondrashov.

Which, of course, is me. Only not me. The ID with my name has Oksana's photo attached.

I suddenly feel a weird link to Oksana that I haven't felt previously. Did she think about me? Was she aware of me in a way that I wasn't of her?

A manager interrupts to tell me that a very young girl came in several weeks ago to ask questions about the guest registry for that same day. Slim, light hair, extremely persistent.

"How old?"

"A child. Maybe eleven? Twelve?"

"You didn't open the registry for her?"

"Of course not."

The manager is lying or misinformed, because Savina Torokhtiy, my mystery caller, could only have obtained my name from this registry. A subsequent search on the internet would have turned up Katya Kondrashov, Kiev Police, and she may have obtained my phone number from the department's City Outreach site.

The anonymous calls to my mobile began soon after.

Finally, I ask, "Do you have parking for the hostel?"

"No, miss."

Okay, no parking, no vehicle plates on record, no Moskvitch to trace. Savina wouldn't have been able to confirm that the hit and run driver was among those on the hostel's list.

Tomorrow it's back to Nikolaev to see Boris Shemetov, who gave the Vitalux receipt to Savina Torokhtiy, age twelve. But why?

Our friend Boris likes to graze greener pastures, the question is, how green does he like them?

****

The next morning, I return to the bee farm.

Boris is harvesting honey, suited up with netting and gloves, the bee smoker at hand. I call out. He pretends he doesn't hear me until I snag a green pear from an overhanging branch and lob it in his direction. It strikes him between the shoulder blades, and he stops in the process of replacing a frame and turns my way.

I approach cautiously. When I'm in conversational range I tell him who stole his car, and that both teenagers are now dead. I describe the girl at the hostel.

"You gave the receipt to Savina Torokhtiy."

"You're mistaken."

"People are turning up dead. Yesterday another girl tried to kill herself."

"It has nothing to do with me."

He pushes past me angrily, I lose my balance, stumble against a hive. It tilts. For a minute nothing happens, and I think I'm safe. Then a whirlwind erupts.

I've never known such absolute, overwhelming fear. It's worse than any pain. It shouldn't exist. The pain of bee stings is nothing in comparison.

But it's bad enough.

I scramble through the buckwheat, flailing my hands. An arm blocks me, and jets of scented smoke flow over me. Boris leads me out of the orchard toward the house, where he examines the damage, and brushes the imbedded stingers away with his fingertips.

"People make too much fuss over a bee sting," he tells me.

Boris father appears at a window, and beckons us inside. Cold compresses follow, and a cup of Ivan Chai. I'm offered honey to go with the herbal tea, but decline.

Twenty minutes later I've recovered enough to be on my way, but first Boris leads me to the garage, where he lifts an old brown tarp. Beneath lies a ruined bicycle. The rear wheel is bent double, the chain is mangled.

"Mrs. Torokhtiy dropped it off, back when I was on the hook for the accident. Said I should get whatever enjoyment I could. Pure malice."

I think, *Not malice. Just pain.*

"Later the girl showed up alone, riding her green and black GT bike."

Savina.

"She said the thieves would leave their fingerprints in the car, and we could catch them."

He shakes his head. "I assured her the police had scoured it. She badgered until I mentioned the Vitalux receipt. She said we should go together and ask the people if they remembered."

He glares at me. "I told her it was impractical, and I sent her home."

****

I return to my hotel.

It's approaching seven o'clock and the western sky glows red and orange. The beach is packed and the parasail hoists another couple aloft. The parasail's fabrics are the Ukrainian colors.

I look on, face and neck swollen by bee venom, arms on fire. A man leads a saddled camel along the sand at water's edge; I assume he's offering rides. The camel's haunches are branded, it's gait is even and deliberate, it's expression sour, and I imagine it hates everything in sight.

My investigation has unraveled. Boris the music teacher was my best guess for perpetrator, but now I'm conflicted. It's true that his reputation was ruined, and his career as a teacher terminated by the accident that killed old Agafa, but his rancor still smolders. Shouldn't he have a different attitude, one of redress, if he'd managed to exact revenge on those responsible?

More to the point, I can't prove a thing.

****

By Wednesday night the effects of the bee attack have moderated, and I purchase tickets to a Dynamos vs. Miners game and invite Dimitri. I'm determined to make up lost ground after the *Très Française* fiasco, but I've miscalculated. Dimitri, a former Dynamo player, is focused on the game and not on me.

I should have anticipated, but I haven't, so I sulk while Dynamos score, and Dimitri notices.

He drapes an arm across my shoulders. "Thanks for this, Katya." He squeezes me playfully. "Is everything okay?" His proximity sparks a small revelation, not only about our relationship, but about the murder of Oksana.

Dimitri's wearing a familiar fragrance. It's the same my brother in law Ilya wore the night Oksana was killed, and I'm sure it's the identical scent I detected in the Mini-Cooper. "Your aftershave's making me fidgety," I tell him. He grins, because he thinks I mean something else. "Just my aftershave?"

"What's it called?"

"Paco Rabanne's One Million."

This is my brother-in-law Ilya's splash-on of choice, and tonight it's Dimitri's too. Someone else wears it as well, and now I remember who.

I need an immediate meeting with Detective Rudskoy, but I can't ditch the game. I've already used the "I'm trying to catch a killer" excuse with Dimitri before, and I imagine it's wearing thin. Besides, Dimitri deserves his due. This isn't the first time he's rendered invaluable aid on a case.

What can I say about my boyfriend that isn't sappy, smitten or trite?

A decade as a Dynamo player – *we love you if you score, hate you if you don't*- has given him a lopsided smile.

His affection is constant but careless, and there's no center to those too-dark eyes.

He's obsessive about his clothes; far more than I, but his hair is too long and somewhat uneven. I think it was cut by gypsies, between swigs of wine.

I lean in and press my lips to his neck. Dimitri's been good for me, and I should start being good for him. Either that, or let him go.

****

I want to fill in the blanks before I talk with Misters Rudskoy and Bumchik, but first there's a negotiation with the parents of Elizaveta by phone. I promise them that my visit to the hospital won't touch on sensitive topics, and that I'll confine myself entirely to events that occurred last summer, concerning Oksana Melnyk. I'm lying, but it's the only way I'll be permitted to see Elizaveta, who remains under observation at Children's Clinical Hospital # 1. I try not to think about the disciplinary hearing I'll be facing if Elizaveta's parents file a complaint.

The hospital is located just north of Anna's, on the far side of Verblyud Gulf. I shoot up Boraterska Street and I'm there in ten.

Elizaveta is listening to an audio book on a Bluetooth headset, and her left arm is heavily bandaged. I'm guessing she cut deep with her knife, which persuades me she's not so fragile after all. I also remind myself that she helped squeeze a dead boy under a chain link gate.

She keeps her headphones on, but I know she can hear me. "You have Sasha Yegoshin's phone, and you've been faking pictures of Sasha in Minsk and texting them to his friends."

Elizaveta looks away, her breathing quickens, and her monitor hiccups.

I pull up a chair. I reach over and tap her headphones, and she shoots me a look that's both anguished and reproving. She is wretched as well as wounded, and she demands my sympathy.

Maybe I'm being too subtle.

I pull out my mobile. "I'm about to call the detectives on this case, and in twenty minutes they'll show up with handcuffs."

That seems to work.

The fiction about Belarus was Oksana's idea, she tells me, to explain Sasha's absence, but that part I've already figured.

The next bit is more bizarre.

Oksana wanted a ceremony on the one-year anniversary of Sasha's death, a sort of improvised funeral. She insisted that Misha and Elizaveta meet her at ten o'clock in the morning at The Crane Graveyard, when Oksana wanted to open the grave and view the remains.

"She was worried about him."

"She wanted to see Sasha's corpse?"

"She wanted to be sure he was alright."

"Well, he wasn't."

"She'd seen a zombie movie and she was convinced he might have mutated. That's why we had to go during the day, when he'd be inactive."

I'm not certain if Elizaveta's making this up, and it must be showing.

"You don't get it," says Elizaveta. "People believe that stuff, even normal people."

"Wasn't she concerned she'd be discovered?"

"The Crane Graveyard's closed on weekends. There's a sign that says 'Inquiries 10 to 5 M-F', with a number."

"It's not closed. In fact, there was a drop-off that same afternoon. Not to mention, other kids go there routinely to hang out."

"It wasn't carefully thought out, obviously."

I'm taken aback by Elizaveta's superior tone, and not sure I like it. "Did you inform anyone you were going to the Crane Graveyard that day?"

"I didn't go. I wasn't going to look at a bunch of old bones."

"But did you tell anyone?"

"No!"

I take a breath. "Why did you hurt yourself?"

Elizaveta's little fox face tightens. "It seemed like an option."

"You could have saved her. You could have told someone."

She sighs, slips off the headphones. She over-enunciates to make herself crystal clear. "I didn't think she'd go to the Crane Graveyard without us. I never imagined anyone would try to harm her."

Sometimes there's nothing useful one can say, and occasionally I have enough presence of mind to remember that. Other times I don't.

"That's a coward's answer."

****

I call Misha Grojsman from my car. Misha insists he didn't tell anyone about the secret ceremony, really, and although I have no clue what constitutes reality for Misha, I decide to believe him.

So what's next?

Only three people knew Oksana Melnyk was going to visit the Crane Graveyard for a makeshift funeral, unless she told someone else.

The secret ceremony was Oksana's effort to make amends, out of guilt and pain. She was frantic to atone. What if she'd tried to make restitution in other ways? What if she reached out to someone?

Clouds part, the sun flashes down. I couldn't figure how the killers were able to track down Oksana, following such a meager trail of crumbs. That's because they couldn't, and they didn't.

I've been tackling this from the wrong end. Oksana's killers didn't find her, she found them.

I call Mrs. Torokhtiy, in Nikolaev, the victim's daughter-in-law.

****

Independence Day, August 24th and it's spitting rain. Armored tanks race by, heading for the parade kick-off. I'm on duty, directing traffic.

Anna and Ilya are taking the mini-Melnyks to the parade for a dose of Ukrainian national fervor. I've barely spoken to my sister in days, but I know that recent events have worn Anna out; she's straining at the frazzled end of her tether.

From experience I've learned that curing Anna's malaise is a straightforward matter of pampering her for a day, and I really should step up, but I'm delaying because I'm enjoying our estrangement. It's a vacation from the child-rearing, husband-managing, TV-obsessing daily carousel that Anna considers real life, which she never stops nattering about.

I hear cannon salutes booming one street over, and thunderous sound effects follow. Artillery blanks? If I didn't know better, I'd think the city was under attack. It sounds like a rocket barrage on Luhansk, which I experience, from a prudent distance, on nightly TV.

I dig into a bag of cottage cheese donuts, and wash two or three down with black tea. It's going to be a long day with no end in sight. My shift on patrol is only the beginning, because I've arranged a sit-down with Detectives Bumchik and Rudskoy this afternoon. I have information on the Oksana Melnyk case, and it's time for full disclosure.

****

Another day and another funeral, but on this occasion the casket is closed. The trees are yellowing at the edges, and red squirrels dart among the headstones.

The Yegoshin's are burying their son.

Mrs. Yegoshin is virtually unrecognizable. Her eyebrows have been inexplicably shaved; her face is an enigmatic mask of white makeup. It's freaky Kabuki. I'm wondering if the death of her son has tipped Mrs. Yegoshin over the precipice.

I'm not close enough to determine whether Mr. Yegoshin is wearing cologne today, but if he is, I'm guessing it's Paco Rabanne. I've been warned to keep my distance, and not to spook them.

As they exit the cemetery the Yegoshins are approached by officers who invite them to present themselves at Police Headquarters, and the Yegoshins go along without a fuss.

****

I'm watching a monitor at HQ.

Sasha Yegoshin's parents aren't cooperating. They didn't rent a dark blue Mini-Cooper and they were never in the proximity of the Crane Graveyard. Mr. Yegoshin keeps his mouth shut, while Mrs. Yegoshin's demeanor vacillates between sullen and spiteful.

"Do you know a woman named Leysa Barkalov?"

"Why would I?"

"She misplaced her driver's license recently. She thinks while shopping at the ECO-market in Voskresenka."

"That's nothing to me."

"Nothing? You manage the ECO-market in Voskresenka, is that correct, Mrs. Yegoshin?"

"I'm rarely there."

"The rental clerk at VIP-U-rent recognized your picture. He's identified you as the woman who rented a Mini-Cooper under the name Leysa Barkalov."

(In fact, this isn't true. I'm told the clerk has a hazy recollection at best.)

"He's mistaken."

Rudskoy shuffles papers. He's shifting strategy, preparing to impeach the Yegoshin's statements.

"Do you know a young lady named Savina Torokhtiy?"

"No."

"She didn't contact you a few weeks ago?"

"Not at all."

Detective Rudskoy elaborates. "Miss Torokhtiy claims she told you that Oksana Melnyk confessed to her she'd buried your son in a junkyard, and that she was going to hold a secret funeral on the anniversary of his death."

Mr. Yegoshin sinks his head in his hands, but Mrs. Yegoshin is steel.

"I've never heard of her. She's a liar."

The Yegoshins continue to deny their involvement, but there's compelling evidence to the contrary. I hit the remote button on monitor two.

****

Yesterday afternoon in Nikolaev, Detective Bumchik recorded a witness interview at the Torokhtiy home. The subject was twelve-year-old Savina, accompanied by her mother Natasha.

"In June, a girl called on Mama's phone."

"You mean the land line."

"Yes. She said she was sorry about my gran. I said, 'That happened a long time ago.'"

"Did she give her name?"

"Oksana."

"And did she say how she'd heard about your grandmother's accident?"

Savina shrugs. "Everyone's heard about it."

"Of course."

 "She called because she was also grieving for a loved one. I asked if her grandmother died, and she said no, someone else.

"I felt so sorry for her. I said if she wanted to talk again she should call my mobile."

I believe Savina did feel sorry, just as I believe that at the moment she's thrilled to be talking to the police, and avid to impress Detective Bumchik. She's wearing short-shorts and a pink t-shirt, and I'm also noticing lipstick, blush, and tiny seashell earrings. Because I know Savina is a clever girl, I'm guessing she's come prepared and rehearsed, and we can expect a surprise.

Oksana Melnyk not only called Savina back, she did so more than forty times.

As the interview proceeds I learn that Oksana, heedless of discretion and desperate to confide in a sympathetic listener, made daily calls to Savina Torokhtiy. With each call, Savina garnered additional details about a boy named Sasha, about the car accident, about the horrifying night on the beach in Kobleve, and the ill-conceived burial in the Crane Graveyard.

Even though she'd already contacted me early on (and accused me of the hit and run), now Savina honed in on the name Alexander "Sasha" Yegoshin, from the list she'd acquired at the Black Sea Hostel. This was the person who'd killed her beloved grandmother Agafa.

Mister Bumchik backtracks. He wants to know if Savina acted independently.

"Who drove you to the hostel in Kobleve?"

"I rode alone on the bus."

"Really? You're a bit young to travel by yourself."

Savina appears puzzled. "I do it all the time." Her mother Natasha interjects a soft denial, while Savina smiles.

In the following days Savina considered her position. She had information that she could use, information that others were desperate to obtain. It didn't seem right to keep it to herself.

Her attempts to reach Mr. Yegoshin at his office were initially met with obstruction. She was transferred, or cut off. Finally, after insisting that Mr. Yegoshin's son had been involved in a car crash, she was put through.

She asked Sasha's father if he knew he'd raised a murderer.

Next she asked whether Yegoshin knew why his son had disappeared.

Mr. Yegoshin didn't know, but was desperate to learn. Savina parceled out what she knew of the hit and run, the drowning, and the plans for the secret funeral on the anniversary of Sasha's death.

Yegoshin wasn't having it. He was insistent that Sasha would never steal a car. If he'd struck a cyclist, he'd stay and call for aid. His boy had a conscience, and had been brought up to value life.

Savina says she saw no reason not to believe him.

On the monitor, she spreads her hands. It's a child's imitation of an adult gesture, but it's charming for that reason. She appeals to Detective Bumchik's impartiality. "Oksana hid Sasha's death to throw off the police, because she didn't want to share the blame. That's what everyone thinks. But we don't know Sasha Yegoshin's side of the story, do we?

"I told the Yegoshins what I believed. Oksana Melnyk was driving the car that killed my grandmother, and she murdered her boyfriend to keep him from telling."

****

Sergeant Dasha takes a seat beside me, and hands me a cola. "She looks like an angel. I wore corrective lenses at that age and I had a double chin."

"The important thing is, you turned out cute," I say.

"What do you think of her story?"

I tilt the cola bottle, swallow, hiccup. "I expected more drama. Sasha Yegoshin rose from his grave at midnight, and Savina witnessed it. Or Oksana let slip where she hid the strychnine."

Sgt. Dasha sniffs. "Our little angel didn't do badly. She made certain that both occupants of the murder car were dead. I expect she'll hone her skills as she gets older."

She pokes me with a finger. "Sorry, I know the Melnyk girl was related."

"No problem."

****

Rudskoy rises and leaves the room as the Yegoshins wait. The next step in the process will include filing charges, and the only remaining issue is whether the couple went to the Crane Graveyard with murder in mind.

I'm not privy to the thoughts of the Yegoshins, but I suspect they drove to the Crane Graveyard to confront Oksana, who refused to concede that Sasha was dead, and balked at showing them Sasha's grave. Mrs. Yegoshin, or perhaps her husband, picked up a loose wedge of cement and slammed it into Oksana's face. Oksana fell backward, struck her head on a section of grated walkway, and died.

This is how I see it. Two grieving parents, provoked by a little girl, committed a dreadful murder, and a tormented teenager, attempting to make amends, met her death in a city junkyard.

Part VI - September

Anna is scowling at the TV, and I'm taking advantage of her distraction to eat the icing she's made for lemon cake. It's September, first day of school, and Tru-Vision is running clips of first-years ringing the opening bell. This should gladden Anna's heart; instead she's downcast.

Our mother has hired a divorce lawyer, the final step that she's never previously reached. This, coupled with the recent death of her sister-in-law Oksana, has blighted Anna's world view. "We don't control anything," she protests. "Why bother getting out of bed?"

I call Lydia Melnyk to mind the kids, and Anna and I catch a tram downtown. I buy her a pair of limited edition sneakers, since she's been coveting mine. This has a minimal effect, but at least she stops sniveling. Next we head around the corner and raid Lvov Handmade Chocolates, while I tell her about my adventures in Nikolaev, with emphasis on the bee attack. Anna's mood visibly improves as I describe my pain and panic.

Finally, I say, "Mom and Dad's divorce is likely for the best - I'm certain they'll both be fine. My only concern is that my sister, Anna Melnyk, is not her lively, buoyant, annoying self."

Major gaffe, as a fresh bout of snuffling ensues. We share a lingering hug on the sidewalk, which is what she wanted in the first place. I've been snared by sticky Anna-angst, like a bug on a sundew plant, and I blame only myself.

She grips my arm as we head for the tram stop. I'm relieved we're not fighting anymore, but I'm also perplexed. I can't fathom Anna's demand for attention, nor her need to be soothed for every grievance. Why yield to the caprices of the heart?

I wish I could say with certainty that I'm not missing out, but in the end it's Anna who's made a family, and it's Anna whom my parents consider an exemplary success. The results of my own efforts are difficult to tally.

I close my eyes and see the seacoast at Kobleve, and a blue and yellow parasail, lit by afternoon sun.

The End

Printed in Great Britain
by Amazon